A Yacht Club Murder Mystery

The Single Shoe Mystery
JANINE MARIE

Book 1

Rigging A Murder Series

This book is a work of fiction. The characters, incidents, and dialogue are drawn from the author's imagination and are not to be construed as real. Any resemblance to actual events or persons, living or dead, is entirely coincidental.

The Single Shoe Mystery

Book one, Rigging A Murder Series

Copyright © 2013 by Chritchley/Ball

ISBN: 978-0-9891848-3-0

FIRST EDITION

To my wonderful family
Thank you for
Your support and inspiration

Janeva Jags unexpectedly finds herself embroiled in the middle of a captivating mystery. On a sailing vacation in a remote inlet off the coast of British Columbia, Janeva finds the peaceful tranquility of this desolate area is shattered when a spontaneous dinner invitation aboard a 100-foot luxury yacht leads to murder. As suspicious events plague Janeva's family, Janeva realizes that only she has the key to solving this mystery and stopping the murderer from killing again.

Dive into the lives of Yacht Club members, in this exciting cocktail of boating, high finance, technology, socialites and trust funds. The result is deadly as passions and greed mix together.

Readers are saying:

"I loved the yacht club setting and the characters were just like old friends. Well Done!"

"Great Setting. This was a fun book to read. Great to read on your yacht, if you have one – or your patio – you can be an armchair sailor. I can't wait for the next one in the series!"

Table of Contents

PROLOGUE ❖

"NO! It can't be!"

"It's time to get up," whispered the handsome twenty-something to his equally attractive crewmember. On this yacht he was first mate, running the boat when required and always making sure it was in tiptop shape. The young woman he was now trying to wake up was his girlfriend and yacht housekeeper.

"What? NO! Its still dark out," came the sleepy female voice in response. "I don't have to be on deck for hours yet, let me go back to sleep— PLEASE."

"Don't roll over... you're not going back to sleep," he urged, gently shaking her. "It's already 5 am! Remember our plans for today, we need to get out of here before anyone sees us."

"5 am! Good God, this is early," she said, sitting up

and rubbing her eyes. "Oh, okay."

"Good! Now get out of bed and get dressed."

"Okay, okay," she groaned, getting out of bed and pulling her clothes on. Not a morning person, she had left her clothes at the end of the bed.

"Drink this."

She smiled gratefully, accepting the steaming mug of coffee and cookie that were being offered.

"There will be enough daylight for us to leave the boat in 10 minutes or so; that gives us just enough time to get organized and leave."

"Right," came the garbled reply through a mouth full of cookie. "I'm ready."

"Good." He peeked out the door at the cook's cabin across the hall. "Nancy is still asleep and the rest of the boat shouldn't be up for a few hours yet. I looked up and down the dock and all the other boats' blinds are down, so, as far as I can tell, if we're quick and quiet we're in the clear."

Putting down her coffee and zipping up her light jacket, she looked around. "Darn; I left my shoes on deck last night."

"Because I love you so much, I grabbed them out of the cockpit shoe box for you. Do all you women HAVE to wear the same style of shoes?" he asked, shaking his head and smiling. "Now hurry up. We don't have much time, we can sneak out the crew door and head straight out to the dock."

"That was sweet of you," she said quietly, taking the shoes, and gave him a quick kiss.

He reached out his hand to take hers and they quietly left their cabin together.

~~~~~~~~~~~~~~~~~~~~~~~~

At 8 am Nancy walked out of her cabin ready to start the day, as cook of the 100-foot yacht Atlantis. Looking across the narrow hallway, she was startled to see the door open. Strange, she thought— normally those two didn't get out of bed until she brought down the breakfast tray. Those two being Carl, the first mate, and Carl's girlfriend Sandy, the housekeeper, who did all the cleaning inside and out, with the exception of the galley, which was Nancy's territory. Nancy checked the crew's galley/salon in case Carl and Sandy were there, but as she expected, it was dark and empty.

Was she late? Were they getting an early start? No... if that was the case they would've been banging on her door to get the coffee going and some hot tea biscuits, the usual fare for a traveling morning. Peeking in Carl and Sandy's cabin, she saw that the bed was empty and unmade. Puzzled, she went up the crew stairs to the main galley, put on coffee, and started to prepare for her day. After getting the tea biscuits in the oven, she went to retrieve the table linens she'd put in the laundry the previous night. Quietly she took the stairway from the galley to the lower level, into a sophisticated foyer paneled with rich wood. She opened the hidden panel door and entered a large laundry room with a full-sized, stacked washer/dryer, storage area, and an ironing station. After filling her basket with tea towels and dishrags, Nancy was heading back up to the galley when something caught her eye down the short hallway leading to the yacht owner Lorenzo's office.

Much to her surprise, light was radiating from Lorenzo's office. Lorenzo kept his office door closed when he was working, and locked otherwise. Curious, she pushed the office door fully open. The grisly sight that met Nancy made her knees buckle. The body lay in a pool of blood, lifeless brown eyes staring at her, arms and legs bent at improbable angles. Dropping to a squatting position on the ground she resisted the urge to scream; instead she turned, scrambled to her feet, and ran to look for help.

Chapter One

Princess Louisa

"Will it be a pink drink or champagne?" inquired Stephanie, my good friend and fellow boater.

"Hmm," I pondered, as I finished cleating off the line that rafted our two boats together. Our boat is a 40-foot sailboat. Stephanie and Greg Writeman, our best friends, have a 54-foot Carver cabin cruiser named Write-Now. This is significant because the shape and size difference between our sailboat and their powerboat make rafting together a challenge, but we've been boating with Stephanie and Greg for many years and have developed a system.

"It's so peaceful," I marveled aloud, as I looked around at the still water. We'd just finished the sometimes-tricky job of anchoring, then rafting our two boats together. "Pink drink—yes, that will be perfect to enjoy with this amazing view," I finally pronounced. Our version of a pink drink is actually a lemon vodka martini with pomegranate juice. Stephanie turned, went inside her boat, and reappeared moments later with a shaker and two glasses in hand.

"What, how did you do that?" I asked, laughing.

"I had a feeling that a pink drink would be perfect to go with that amazing sunset," she said, pointing off to the west.

"Mom, can I go out on the tube?" Katie my beautiful long-blond-haired 11-year-old daughter interrupted.

"Ok, but try not to get wet. It will cool off quickly." Katie loved floating and jumping off the tube. "And tie the tube to the back of the boat: you never know what currents might be under the water's calm surface."

"A beer would hit the spot," my husband Thomas's voice floated back to me from the foredeck, where he was securing the anchor line. "It's thirsty work setting an anchor."

"Can I have a root beer?" Katie asked, giving me her cute look.

"Okay, okay; coming right up!" I called, as I descended the stairs into our sailboat.

A short while later, all the adults were comfortably sitting on the back of our boat, sipping our drinks and listening to Jimmy Buffet.

"Tomorrow we hike the falls first thing," announced my husband in his usual CEO manner, which assumes that everyone will of course do exactly as he expects. This might work well at the office but not so much with family and friends, who are completely immune to his autocratic charms. Katie, who was back on the boat, immediately said, "You promised you'd take me tubing behind Greg and Stephanie's dingy... "

"So you did," laughed Greg. "First we go tubing, then... we go out to Jervis Inlet and drop the prawn trap."

"What about the rapids?" asked Katie.

To get to this secluded paradise, where we were anchored. You need to first, negotiate the Malibu Rapids. The rapids can be very tricky, with narrow turns and a current that can flow as quickly as 10 knots. That might not seem fast to a powerboat like Stephanie and Greg's Carver, but our sailboat only motors at 7 knots. Being seasoned boaters, we always made the trip at slack tide and encountered no trouble.

"Slack tide is at 9:30 tomorrow morning, so we'll go then. Anyway we should really do our tubing away from the other anchored boats so we don't kick up a wake," said Thomas, looking at his tide book and getting into the spirit of things.

My husband and his best friend Greg couldn't look more different; Thomas is 5 feet 10, with thick wavy dark-brown hair and a powerful body. Greg, on the other hand, is well over 6 feet tall and lean, with a mop of straight blond hair falling over his right eye that he's always sweeping back. Both were wearing the unofficial Yacht Club wardrobe of khaki shorts, blue and white nautical shirts, baseball hats, and Patagonia jackets. This type of fleece jacket is a must in the Pacific Northwest, especially in Canada, where we were cruising this year.

Over the stereo Jimmy Buffet sang:

> Cheeseburger in paradise
> Medium rare with mustard
> Be nice Heaven on earth with an onion slice
> I'm just a cheeseburger in paradise
> I like mine with lettuce and tomato
> Heinz 57 and french-fried potatoes
> Big kosher pickle and a cold draft beer
> Well good God almighty
> which way do I steer
> for my cheeseburger in paradise?

"... Good God almighty, which way do I steer for my cheeseburger in paradise," sang out Thomas and Greg.

"Okay, I get the hint! Steph, I'll make the burgers, will you make a salad?" I asked across the boats.

"You're on!"

We both disappeared to start our dinner preparations.

"Janeva, honey," came Thomas's voice, in that well-known tone that means If you really love me you will drop what you are doing and get me a...

"Our beers are broken... "

One of the secrets to a happy marriage, I have learned, is not to point out at this point that they are sitting in the sun doing nothing while I am busy preparing dinner. The best solution is to smile and say, "Here you go" as I hand up two more Coronas with lime wedges and take the empties to store for future recycling. The downside of anchoring is that you have to store all your garbage and recycling until you get to the next marina that will take it for you, usually for a price, especially if it's an island, since they have to pay to have it barged off to the mainland.

After a yummy cheeseburger dinner, we lit tea lights and settled down to watch the stars come out. Katie, Steph, and I spent a pleasant time with a Star Finder wheel, trying to identify constellations. But all good things must come to an end, and it was almost 11 pm—definitely time for Katie's bedtime, not to mention mine.

~~~~~~~~~~~~~~~~~~~~~~~

"What is the rest of the world doing?" mused Thomas as we sat on the back of the boat enjoying coffee in the early morning sun.

"I love this time of day; it's so peaceful. What kind of bird do you think that is?" I replied, pointing at a small black duck-like bird with a bright yellow beak floating on the calm water that shimmered in the sun, reflecting the mountains that surrounding our anchorage.

Ignoring the question, or perhaps taking it as rhetorical, Thomas continued as if I hadn't spoken: "Halcyon; yes, that's what today is— halcyon."

"Probably a black scoter,' said Katie, looking up from her book and glancing at the bird in question. "When are we going prawning?"

"Ask Greg, it's his dingy."

"But they're still in bed!"

"Then you'll have to wait."

Fortunately for the brooding 11-year-old Katie, just then Greg emerged from his boat to stretch and wish us a good morning.

"Did I hear you're ready to go catch some prawns for dinner tonight?" he teased her

"Oh yes, I'm ready! When do we cast off, Skipper?" replied Katie.

"I need coffee and muffin, then we're off. Who else is coming?"

"Not me," I instantly replied. "I'm going to enjoy this amazing morning reading and drinking great quantities of coffee to balance the great quantities of wine I drank last night."

"I'm with Janeva," came the sleepy voice of Steph from inside.

"Thomas?" Greg asked.

"What? Let the Skipper go out without Gilligan?" replied Thomas, reluctantly looking up from his iPad, where he was desperately trying to connect to the Internet to get his morning papers.

Laughing, I said, "Please, please take him away. The lack of cell coverage and, worse, no Wi-Fi is making Thomas a grumpy boy."

Soon they were off in the dingy to get our prawn dinner and go tubing. I sent them with extra towels and settled down to do some reading.

~~~~~~~~~~~~~~~~~~~~~~~~

"Mom, we went sooo fast!" Katie's excited voice broke through my dozing. Sigh; so much for reading. The gentle rocking of the boat and soft warmth of the day, birdsong and the lapping of small waves on the boat, the quiet peacefulness of the morning had overwhelmed me, and I had fallen asleep.

"Mom, it was really fun to go through the rapids in the dingy EVEN though it was slack tide. There were so many boats leaving, and you can't see around the bend so you can't pass."

I looked around the placid 5-mile basin that makes up the anchoring area under the falls, as Katie talked on so rapidly I don't think she had time to breathe. I was surprised to see how empty the basin was; the night before it had been packed with anchoring boats. We had felt lucky to find enough space for us to raft together; the shore was full of boats anchored with stern lines to keep them from swinging with the tide and colliding with each other.

"Then," continued Katie, catching her breath and holding up a can of cold Mugs root beer from the cooler as I nodded a "Yes" to the unspoken question of can I have the soda? "We found the perfect spot to put down the prawn trap. We were really careful to check the depth on the fish finder AND to make a waypoint on the GPS, so Dad can't lose this trap," she finished laughing and opening up her soda. I laughed too, as Thomas had a longstanding reputation for losing prawn traps.

"We will see tomorrow," I replied laughing.

"How about hiking the falls now?" asked Thomas, in a way that we knew wasn't really a question. "I could use some exercise after being on the boat all day yesterday; it's a long day getting up here."

"Do we have to?" whined Katie, who as a rule didn't like long walks or hikes.

"How about I pack a picnic?" I suggested.

"Great idea," Steph chimed in.

Katie looked around at the group. Realizing she was outnumbered, she decided to make the best of it. "Okay... if we can have some Cliff Bars."

"Done! Now come and help me make the lunch," I replied quickly, before she could come up with any other qualifiers.

Chapter Two

Chatterbox Falls

"Katie, grab what you want to drink on the hike and any granola bars you want, and pass them to me, please. I believe we are ready to go," I said, as I zipped up the specially designed picnic knapsack. It is a great knapsack with a section for dishes, plastic glasses, and napkins, including a separate insulated section for food and drinks.

"Ahoy there." A small dingy with a man wearing a Tilly hat pulled up to the sterns of our boats. I poked my head out of the companionway, but both Greg and Thomas had waved and it looked like Greg, who knows everyone at the Yacht Club, knew him.

"Hi Trent, I don't see your boat anywhere," said Greg in his amiable way. "Thomas, this is Trent."

"Trent Braise-Bottom the Third, at your service," corrected Trent, lifting his Tilly hat in a formal manner not used since the turn of the century and nodding to Thomas.

"Always nice to meet a fellow Yacht Club member," countered Thomas, making a visible effort not to laugh.

"That lovely new Tiara 4300 Open series anchored over there is new to me this season. Isn't she a beauty?" said Trent, pointing to a shiny new powerboat anchored off to the left of us. After receiving the appropriate nods and sounds of appreciation from Thomas and Greg, he went on, "It's so comfortable that even Wiffy loves it! We have been here for a week, but the weather is changing so we are leaving tomorrow morning at slack tide. The boat's got everything but a cook and Wiffy is desperate to go out for dinner," he laughed, taking a moment to grab the side of our boat so he didn't drift off as he had cut his engine. "Have you been to the falls yet?"

"Not yet, but we're about to hike them and have a picnic as soon as Mom is done making it," interceded Katie.

"Do you know the story of the falls?" Getting a wide-eyed "No" from Katie, he went on, "Well, Wiffy and I come up here for a several weeks every year; this is a special place for us. So I make it my job when we are here to welcome other Yacht Club members and act as kind of an ambassador, sharing my special knowledge of this incredible area.

Would you like me to tell you about it?" he asked Katie, though we were all on deck now listening to his narrative. "The falls," he turned and pointed in their direction, "are named Chatterbox Falls, and these magnificent tree-lined cliffs that surround us are granite, this gorge we are anchored in was originally cut by a glacier, and those granite cliffs I just showed you rise to heights in excess of 2,100 meters."

A glance told me that Katie was doing some quick multiplication in her head. "So these cliffs are like 6,300 feet high... wow," she said, in awe.

Looking a little put out at the interruption in his lecture, Trent continued, "In mid-June, the warm sun melting the mountain snow creates more than sixty rivers and waterfalls that combine to cascade down precipitous walls to the waters of Princess Louisa Inlet below. Tumbling 45 meters—

"Or 135 feet," interrupted Katie—

"called Chatterbox Falls." Trent continued.

"Princess Louisa Inlet, or Suivoolot to the Native Indians, meaning 'Sunny and Warm,' has beckoned sea travelers since it was first seen by man. Except for aircraft, the sea is the only way here. The only public road is 40 miles away; it's not even accessible by 4-wheel drive. The privilege of enjoying this bit of paradise" —waving his arms around like a preacher at this point, Trent almost fell out of his dingy in his enthusiasm—"comes through the generosity and foresight of James F. (Mac) MacDonald, who first saw Princess Louisa

Inlet in 1919. He learned of the inlet from an uncle who had sailed to it in 1907. Mr. MacDonald remembered the spectacular beauty of the inlet as he traveled throughout the world. In 1926, after years of prospecting in Nevada, Mac struck it rich. With his newfound riches, he was able to attain his real Eldorado, or Princess Louisa Inlet. He purchased the land surrounding Chatterbox Falls in 1927 and built a log cabin. Unfortunately it was tragically destroyed by fire in 1940 but has since been rebuilt to a degree. For years, Mac acted as host to visiting yachtsmen and sailors."

Here Trent changed his voice from a British accent to what he perceived as an old raspy American gold miner and continued on, quoting old Mac:

"This beautiful, peaceful haven should never belong to one individual," he said. "I don't ever want it to be commercialized. Indians, trappers, loggers, fishermen and yachtsmen have always been welcome to any hospitality I had to offer. I have felt that I was only the custodian of the property for Nature, and it has been my duty to extend every courtesy."

Switching back to his normal British accent, Trent continued.

"In 1972, in his 83rd year, Mac spent his last summer at the Inlet. He died in 1978.

"To maintain the perpetual trust, the non-profit Princess Louisa International Society was formed with an equal number of Canadian and American trustees. The formation of this society ensured the preservation of this enchantingly beautiful place for all future generations.

"After ten years of careful guardianship, the Princess Louisa International Society, with the blessing of Mr. MacDonald, decided that for greater public benefit, administration of the property should pass to the Government of the Province of British Columbia. With the understanding that all previous stipulations would remain in effect, the property became Princess Louisa Provincial Marine Park in 1965. The Princess Louisa International Society continues to play an active role in the conservation and management of the park."

We all sat enjoying this interesting and informative but clearly memorized lecture from a guidebook for a few moments as we tried to think of what to say next. Finally Katie broke the silence with, "Well, let's go and see this great waterfall, then."

"You need to be very careful, young lady," Trent said solemnly. "Eight hikers have slipped and fallen to their deaths over the years. Make sure you stay on the trail. It's a dangerous two-hour hike to the trapper's cabin."

A bit unnerved and not wanting to frighten Katie, we all laughed and thanked Trent, who, it turned out, wasn't done with us quite yet:

"The real reason I came over was to …"

We exchanged looks. Was he about to start on yet another 20-minute lecture?

"Make sure you have enough scope out for your

anchor," he continued, "because the weather's changing and I have 5 to 1 anchor line out, and so, depending on what you have... we don't want to swing into each other tonight when the wind kicks up."

"Dad, what is scope?" Katie asked.

"Scope refers to the length of line or chain between the anchor and the boat's bow relative to the depth of water and the weather conditions in which the boat is anchored. Thus, a scope of 3 to 1 indicates that a boat lying in 10 feet of water has an anchor line 30 feet long," Thomas replied.

I tuned out at this point, as the amount of anchor chain out is not my area. Gathering up the knapsack I had filled I started to load up the dingy, lock up our boat, and generally make ready to go. Thomas and Greg managed to convince Trent that his boat was safe from us and that we had sufficient but not too much anchor out to ride out the weather change, and we got in the dingy and made for shore.

~~~~~~~~~~~~~~~~~~~~~~~~~~

The hike was beautiful, huge fir trees and ferny underbrush, with the sun shining through the breaks in the tall trees, turning the hike into an almost surreal fairy landscape of different shades of green floating on the mist from the waterfall. The trail was steep, definitely steeper than I had anticipated, and we were all out of breath by the time we found the perfect fallen log (it was huge) on which to enjoy our picnic. We were too tired to go up higher, plus it seemed to be getting darker, which was very strange because it was only three in the afternoon.

We decided to head back down the trail. In a clearing we noticed that the sun had disappeared and it was getting cloudy. The growing darkness but made us even more eager to get down as it was slippery from the waterfall spray and getting hard to see.

Finally we emerging from the trees. As we made our way to the dock, we noticed a thick fog had rolled in. We were hot and sweaty from our exertions but there was a definite chill or, more specifically, dampness in the air.

"I think it's going to rain," I said.

"Looks like it; let's get back to the boat," Thomas replied.

"The wind is building too... how about we move the boats to the visitor dock for the night while there is still room?" said Greg, looking around.

Thomas nodding in agreement and looking around at the other boats mused "Good thinking, and we better hustle or we won't get a spot. It's not an original idea. Look: Trent's Tiara is already on its way here, and so is that other Yacht Club boat. Janeva, Katie, and Steph—why don't you girls hang out on the dock to catch us and hold a spot for us if you can, and we'll bring the boats over?"

As we watched them leave in the dingy, it started to rain. We looked around for cover, and not finding any we started to walk back up the dock to stand under a large fir tree to get what cover it could provide. Fortunately it hadn't started to rain in earnest and we were able to stay reasonably dry until we saw Trent Braise-Bottom the Third coming in on his new Tiara.

"I guess we had better go and help him," I moaned.

Laughing, Steph replied, "Yup. Look at his wife, or should I say Wiffy? She is so bundled up she will never get off the boat in time to catch his lines."

"Katie, why don't you stay here and keep dry?"

"Sounds good to me" was her quick reply, as she rummaged through the backpack looking for another granola bar or other treat. "Can I have... ?" trailed after me as Steph and I ventured out in the now pouring rain.

"Yes," I yelled back, knowing there was only one Cliff Bar and an apple left in the backpack.

After catching and securing Trent's Tierra to the dock, we were just in time to catch our two boats. As we were now thoroughly drenched we took ourselves below to change into dry clothes and dry off.

Chapter Three

Dinner on a Hat

Finally I was feeling warm again! Curled up in my favorite yoga pants and under a fleece blanket drinking a cup of tea, I flipped through the pages of our DVD collection book. To save space I had removed them from their cases and put them in a book, four to a page. Of course it would have been prudent to put them in alphabetical order, or any sort of order for that matter. Hmmm. After giving this some thought I decided that that was one of those excellent projects that other people did.

Katie and Thomas were busy suggesting DVDs that I don't even think we owned as I rapidly flipped the pages in gathering frustration. Finally I randomly picked a disk and put it in the player.

Fortunately I was saved by the timely arrive of Greg

and Steph from what would otherwise have been a rather embarrassing "Did you really pick that DVD?" moment as the Flintstones' theme song, "Flintstones / Meet the Flintstones / They're a modern Stone Age fam-i-lee" started to blast through the speakers.

"We come bearing gifts," announced Greg

"I love the Flintstones, and I have popcorn," sang Steph, as she waved around two full popped bags of microwave popcorn.

"Wilma!! I'm home!!... " Came the booming voice of Fred Flintstone from the TV.

"Who wants a hot chocolate?" I asked to no one in particular. "I think someone is knocking on our boat," said Thomas loudly, as he maneuvered his way around the crowded galley and headed up the companionway stairs to look out.

"Greg, we need to move our boats." This statement finally had the effect of stopping the multi-way conversation going on between Steph and me about hot chocolate preparation methods, Greg and Katie debating who should hold the bags of popcorn, and Fred and Barney yelling at each other on the TV.

"What?" Greg looked at Thomas, perplexed.

"It's Trent. He says a big Yacht Club boat is coming in and we need to make space."

"Okay." Greg grabbed his foul weather coat and handed Thomas his. Steph grabbed hers and followed them out. "Pause your show, Katie. I have to turn the AC power off for a moment."

We successfully moved our boats and helped Trent move his, with all our boats tied up on the inside, leaving the outside of the dock open for the new boat.

"Its huge," I said in awe, watching the new boat arrive. "Will it fit?"

"Its a 100 feet and will just fit in the space; well, actually it might hang out a bit," said Trent smugly, obviously pleased that he knew the owners of such a fine yacht.

The huge yacht came in with what can only be called as a perfect docking job. We helped tie her up and were heading back to our boat in the forlorn hope that Katie had left us some popcorn when—

"Thank you, and wait!" came a booming voice from above. We looked up to see a man, large but not fat, more solid, with big shoulders and that round protruding belly that looks like they are seven months pregnant that some men get. His hair was dark and wavy in a luxuriant, disheveled way. Waving to us to stay where we were, he made his way down from the command bridge to the back deck to talk to us. We were all curious so we just stood quietly waiting, until he finally walked out the sliding glass doors to the back deck and leaned on the rail of his yacht to speak to us. I think we were all wondering the same thing—was this the hired captain or the owner? Yet as soon as this man had stepped out it was clear that he was the owner, and by his docking job in wind, current, pelting rain, and very little visibility, it was clear that he knew how to run his boat... pardon me, I should say yacht, as a 100-foot Hatteras is definitely a yacht.

"Hi Trent," came the accented deep voice. "Thank you all for being so kind in moving your boats. I know the maximum size is 55 feet and I can't thank you enough for being so accommodating, it's my wife you see, she doesn't enjoy boating." He stopped there, as if that was a reasonable explanation for the huge boat needing to tie up to a dock. These boats can easily ride out storms, especially in such a protected basin as we were in. They have water makers and loud generators, as they require tons of power to run all their electronics.

"You are all Yacht Club members," he continued looking at our dropping wet burgees dropping in the rain.

"Yes, I'm Thomas Jags," said my husband, "and this is my wife Janeva and our good friends Greg and Stephanie Writeman," breaking the silence that this man's presence seemed to uncharacteristically induce in us.

"Always a pleasure to meet fellow Yacht Club members," he said in an accent I now recognized as Italian. "My name is Lorenzo and I insist you all join us for dinner tonight."

"Thank you, but we couldn't possibly," started Steph.

"No, I insist. Our cook is excellent and we have

plenty of food."

"What time?" asked Trent eagerly, clearly not wanting us to talk Lorenzo out of his generous offer.

"Excellent, Trent! I look forward to seeing your lovely wife again." Looking at his watch, the big Italian pronounced, "See you all at 7 pm" with finality and turned to leave. I realized that he had taken Trent's reply to speak for us all.

"Excuse me, Lorenzo, but we have an 11-year-old daughter," I ventured to say.

"Good. I'll have the Wii set up for her." he replied over his shoulder as he walked away.

We turned back to our boats feeling a bit stunned. It was like being summoned!

Back on Greg and Stephanie's boat we crowded around the Yacht Club yearbook to find out Lorenzo's last name.

"Who is he," asked Thomas, "and how did he make his fortune?"

"Italian" was all I could think to add.

"He knows how to run his boat," added Greg with appreciation

"Well I don't know about you, but if we're going for dinner on a yacht tonight I'm going to have a shower and do my hair," I said, running a hand over my wet head.

"Groan…what will we wear?" Steph added.

"The best I have is a sundress," I laughed, thinking of the pouring rain.

Later, Steph and I surveyed each other. We had shared various scarves and jewelry, and were rather pleased with the result.

"You look very elegant," said Steph as I spun around for inspection. "Definitely the brown flip flops" she finished.

I had borrowed a tan sweater to go over the thin straps of my brown-and-gold Tommy Bahama sundress, added a silver necklace, and put my hair up, since no matter how much I tried it still looked frizzy from all the rain. But the end result was surprisingly good.

"So do you," I replied surveying her up and down. "That dress really looks great on you. I think I'll have to give it to you now because it has never looked like that good on me!" I had loaned Steph a straight, ankle-length grey sundress. She had added a folded dark blue sarong over her shoulders and looked great. People often remark that Steph and I could be sisters. We're about the same height, and we both have medium-length light brown hair with the obligatory highlights; the main difference is that Steph is a few years older than I am and where I have soft curves she is lean and athletic.

~~~~~~~~~~~~~~~~~~~

"Permission to come aboard!" Greg yelled, as we boarded the aft deck of the big Hatteras.

"Welcome, come and meet my friends," Lorenzo

bombed, gesturing to us. "We are having cocktails in the cockpit, ha ha ha," he laughed at his own joke. "And just look at that rainbow," he added. We all turned to see a partial rainbow poking in and out of grey clouds. "This is my wife, Catherine," he said as he put his large hand on a delicate, almost waif-like woman. Her long, wavy blond hair only added to the surreal quality about her. She looked up and smiled at us, then turned to fill two champagne glasses with, I noticed, a very nice vintage Dom Perignon. She handed one to me and one to Steph. She turned to refill her own glass; then, noticing Katie, she gave the girl a sweet smile and said, "I bet you like movies?" Katie nodded enthusiastically, so Catherine continued, "Would you like to see our media room? We even have a Wii if you like video games." Katie looked to me and I nodded that she could go with Catherine.

I turned my attention back to Lorenzo, who was busy introducing the everyone: "Traveling with us are Stella and John Blackwood, our good friends from Boston, and I believe you are already acquainted with Trent and his lovely wife."

"Darn," I whispered to Steph. "I guess he doesn't know her real name, either. Wiffy... could that really be her given name? Maybe it's short for something?"

"Wifferina?" Steph giggled in a whisper.

Lorenzo said, "Now sit, please." He gestured us over to a comfortable outdoor seating area with several sofas and chairs, propane heaters, fleece blankets, and an abundance of throw pillows. The others shifted around to let Steph and me sit together. Lorenzo continued to stand, holding court, telling a detailed story of a lucrative past business deal that he and John Blackwood had worked on. Thomas, who follows all business news, jumped in with intelligent questions, leaving the women to visit.

"I have to admit this is lovely," I said, breaking the silence of the group. What a hard crowd. Wiffy said nothing, Catherine, who had returned, looked distracted and more interested in her champagne than us, but fortunately Stella Blackwood leaned toward Steph and me, saying, "Oh, I agree, I love this weather. It's so dramatic."

"Isn't it, though? I can't believe it was pouring rain just a half hour ago and it's so calm now. Just look how the fog sits and swirls above the flat calm water," I agreed.

We three turned to look at the beautiful scene.

"The shades of grey are amazingly pretty, there are so many of them. Just look at the sky, over there it's dark grey almost black, then here light grey closer to us, with every shade of grey you can imagine if you include the mountains, water, and fog," I said.

"It is really spectacular," Steph agreed. "Let's toast to Mother Nature." We held up our glasses and toasted.

"Don't you just love these shoes?" Stella said to Wiffy. We all looked down to see the two had on identical white shoes.

Wiffy simply replied, "Yes, they are great," then looked down shyly at her feet.

"It's so hard to find good boat shoes. These are the best, with white soles that don't mark the deck, they're really lightweight, and this mesh lets them breathe so you can wear them without socks," Stella continued on about the shoes.

Looking down, I had to agree. "Wow, all that and they look good, too! I'll have to get myself a pair. Where did you get them, Stella?"

"John bought them for me. He is so sweet, he is always picking up little thoughtful things for me."

Not knowing what to say to that, I said instead, "What a beautiful flower arrangement." as I reached for a coaster to put down my glass of champagne.

"Yes, we are very fortunate right now, the girl who does our housekeeping is talented that way," said Lorenzo, who had broken away from the cluster of men and moved to stand beside his wife.

He then announced, "On that note, let's all move inside. I think the rain is going to start up again and I believe our talented cook Nancy has prepared a fine meal for us this evening." We all stood up, getting ready to move inside the yacht.

"May I request that you all remove your shoes? Lorenzo suddenly asked, holding up his hand to stop us. "With this wet weather, that's easier on the staff and the carpet," he said with a smile, as he and Catherine removed their shoes and placed them in a box labeled "SHOES." We all followed their example, then moved as a group to the far end of the magnificent salon where an elegant table for 10 was laid out with Royal Crown Derby china and Waterford crystal wine glasses.

"Please take a seat, but please don't sit beside your spouse... it doesn't make for good conversation," said Lorenzo with a wave and a big laugh.

What followed was a lovely dinner of:

Rack of Lamb with Rosemary and Mustard Cream,
Mashed Potatoes with Whole Grain Mustard and Horseradish,
Green Beans with Garam Masala

Adding to the pure joy of an amazing meal was the perfectly paired wine and plenty of it.

Lifting a yummy California Pinot Noir, Lorenzo said "Cin-cin... to the Yacht Club!"

"Salut!" we replied, raising our glasses.

"To the Queen... and cheerio," from Trent.

"To new friends," from Thomas.

"Cheers to Lorenzo's excellent cook," from John, and it went on from there.

How they managed to get so much California wine across the border I will never know, but I wasn't complaining. We had managed to find some lovely BC wine but were having trouble keeping it stocked up, especially as we were provisioning at small remote island general stores. In BC you can only buy wine in government liquor stores, and they aren't that easy to find when you're on a boat. The general stores often have a liquor section (though it's unclear how that works when the large food stores are not allowed to sell alcohol). But the wine selection of these small stores is usually local or of the inexpensive variety.

As the dinner progressed and more and more wine was poured we discovered that Lorenzo was an Italian count, clearly with oodles of money. He spent part of every year in Italy managing family affairs. He had only recently purchased this yacht, spent the winter exploring the Caribbean, and then had the yacht delivered to Seattle because he had always wanted to see Desolation Sound. His wife was not fond of anchoring and boating so he had recently joined the Yacht Club because he wanted use of its many outstations. The Archipelago Yacht Club that we are all members of operates nine outstations for the exclusive use of members. Most outstations offer power, water, ice, laundry, and wireless internet service. All locations offer secure moorage during the summer months.

Lorenzo was clearly the host, with his big personality and booming infectious laugh, but it was John who moved the conversation skillfully from one topic to the next. He was very charming with his blond hair flipped over to one side, his jaunty sweater and Dockers; he could have been a Yacht Club poster boy. His smile and genuine interest brought everyone out, and soon we were all talking and laughing like old friends

The evening's topics included the interesting work that Greg and Steph have been doing for the past few years. Greg is a highly qualified and sought-after physician and Steph a well-known environmental blog writer. After Steph came into an inheritance they both quit their jobs and now volunteer their services to organizations like Doctors without Borders and the World Health Organization, to name just a few. Each year they go with teams of doctors and nurses to do what they can for the sufferers in Third World countries. They had recently returned from Honduras, where hurricanes had caused mass flooding. Greg enjoys putting his medical talents to work helping and caring for the suffering and Steph continues to blog, but now she is writing to increase awareness of Third World countries.

The conversation then flowed to the global recession, the euro crisis, the U.S. "fiscal cliff" and debt ceiling, and the Affordable Care Act. We had just launched into a debate about corporate spying—in particular, about Huawei, a Chinese company that the House of Representatives' Intelligence Committee had asked American companies to stop doing business with, warning that China could use equipment made by the company to spy on certain communications and threaten vital systems through computerized links—when the dessert arrived. It was tiramisu, a generous portion of mascarpone cheese topping espresso-soaked ladyfingers, with a heavy covering of fine cocoa blanketing the top. John noticed that Catherine and Wiffy looked bored so he moved the conversation to Pinterest, an online pin board that appeals to women. This started a lively discussion as the men wanted to know what made it so interesting. I had to admit to spending many hours surfing around Pinterest.

~~~~~~~~~~~~~~~~~~~~~~~~~~~~

"Mom, I'm tired." Katie had come up behind me. Nancy the cook had fed her dinner in the kitchen and she had finished watching a movie in the media room.

Looking at my watch, I saw that it was already 11 pm. "Thank you for the WONDERFUL dinner and the great conversation, but I'm afraid it's well past Katie's bedtime, so I'll take my leave," I said, excusing myself and taking Katie's hand.

"What do you say?" I whispered to her.

She turned and said a very pretty "Thank you" to Lorenzo.

Thomas, Greg, and Steph had also decided to call it a night so we all left together.

It was only as I left that I realized that Katie hadn't said thank you to Lorenzo's wife… what was her name anyway? Too much wine, I guess. Tomorrow we would make up a nice thank-you card and drop it off on their boat early, before everyone left.

Chapter Four

Then Came the Rain

"Mom, I'm hungry," Katie whined the following morning.

"There is fruit and cereal... you know where the galley is. I'm still sleeping," I whined back at her. Actually my head hurt from all the wine last night and I could hear the rain falling on the deck above me. I couldn't find any good reason to get out of my warm bed until—

"Coffee?" said Thomas, who had managed to sneak out to check the lines on this rainy and windy morning and had returned with a thermos full of coffee from Steph and Greg. Now, this was the one thing that could get me out of bed!

"Yes, PLEASE," I replied thankfully. After 15 years of marriage I well knew that I wouldn't be getting the coffee in bed. Taking that fragrant beverage in hand, I asked, "What were you doing up so early?"

"The rain and wind woke me up, so I thought I would check the lines and go for a walk... but there is nowhere to walk to."

I gave him that "Really?" look.

"Okay I admit it, I was trying to see if I could get any cell coverage to download the New York Times on my iPad. No go... I even tried to stand under Lorenzo's boat in hopes that he might have WiFi."

Laughing, I said, "Being out of touch is killing you, isn't it? But I'm sure they must have WiFi on that boat; why don't you just ask?"

"Well, Lorenzo did promise us a tour...perhaps I'll just bring my iPad along," Thomas replied, looking at that item as if he could conjure up the Internet.

"Why is there a wet shoe on the table?" I asked, finally noticing—as the coffee started to work its magic and clear my brain—there was a very wet white shoe sitting on a paper towel right in the middle of the table.

"I found it floating by the dock," chimed in Katie, looking up from the book she was reading.

"What? You went out in the rain, too?" I asked.

"Yup."

"Found one wet shoe and decided to bring it back to our boat?"

"Yup," came the infuriating monosyllabic answer,

so I tried an open-ended question:

"Why did you bring it back here?"

"Don't know, just seemed like the right thing to do."

"Why were you out in the rain this morning?"

"I went out with Dad, but came back when he went over to Greg and Stephanie's boat."

"More coffee, please," I said, holding out my cup to a snickering Thomas, who kindly filled it up for me.

"You are not a morning person!"

"Thanks, Einstein. You would think you would know that by now!"

"What's for breakfast?" asked Thomas sweetly.

Grumbling, I went to the galley and started to prepare some bacon, eggs, and toast.

"Can we move the shoe?" I asked sarcastically as I set the table for breakfast.

Katie picked the shoe up and put it under the bottom stair of the companionway with the rest of our shoe collection.

After the breakfast dishes were done, Thomas and I went over to Greg and Stephanie's boat while Katie settled down to watch Gilmore Girls, Season 2. Katie and I love Gilmore Girls and have all the seasons on DVD. I think Katie relates to the daughter character, "Rory," who is shy and academic just like Katie is. I would love to be able to say I was like "Lorelai," the mom on the show, who is young and hip and always has something clever and witty to say. Hmmm, maybe if I had Amy Sherman-Palladino writing for me, too, I just might. With the theme song from Gilmore Girls playing in the background, I headed over to the Writemans' boat.

Our boat being a sailboat, the living space down below is especially dark in the rain and gloom, whereas Greg and Steph's boat a Carver Voyager, has the galley and living space up with lots of large windows, is as close to bright and cheerful as you can get in the pouring rain. Less private, true, but in this weather, when you couldn't be outdoors, it was nice to be able to see what was happening on the docks, and watch the rain or look for any breaks in clouds. Unfortunately, today there was very little chance of the latter.

"Should we leave?" I asked the group at large.

"Probably. With those high cliffs, the clouds get trapped here. It might not be as bad outside this basin," Thomas replied.

"When is slack tide?"

Greg rummaged around and pulled out the tide table, running his finger down the page "9:54 am." Checking his watch he added, "That's in 35 minutes."

"That would explain all the boats pulling off the dock…look, there goes Trent's boat," mused Thomas as he looked out the window. "Yes, let's leave; I have no wish to sit in the rain any longer," he continued.

I got up, having been married long enough to know that when Thomas says "Let's leave" he means right now! And even though there was no wind at the moment, I've also sailed long enough to know that at the slightest sign of wind Thomas will have the sails up and we will heel over, so anything not properly stowed will go flying from one side of the boat to the other... that is, until we tack, when it will unceremoniously return to its original side of the boat, though probably no longer in its original unbroken condition.

I had just opened the sliding glass door that leads from the spacious airy salon of Greg and Steph's boat onto their back deck when,

'Help! Help!" came a women's cry from the dock

Looking out, I saw Nancy, the cook from Lorenzo's big Hatteras, the Atlantis, who had prepared the delicious dinner for us all the previous night, running frantically up and down the dock screaming.

"What's wrong?" I yelled to her back.

She turned so quickly that she almost slipped on the wet dock. Catching her balance through sobs, she cried, "It's Mr. Moretti, Lorenzo Moretti. Something's wrong! Please come! I need help!" She looked up at us, as we were all now on the back deck looking, continuing to sob, shaking, and clearly very distressed. Greg, who had spent time as an ER doc before retiring, was the first to react.

"Steph, can you grab my medical bag?" he asked

calmly over his shoulder— though unnecessarily, since Steph was already doing so—as he disembarked and walked toward the girl.

"Breathe, take a deep breath.... Now, we need you to show us where Mr. Moretti is," he said to the girl, looking her in the eye and oozing with a calm professional manner that instantly helped the girl get enough control of her panic to lead the way.

We all followed her, except for Katie, who, hearing the cry, had managed to pull herself away from her DVD and had come up on the deck our sailboat. But I instructed her to stay on our boat and promised I would let her know what had happened as soon as I knew myself. She looked rebellious and tried to protest but a look from her father sent her back down the companionway.

Running now to catch up with the fast-moving group as they boarded the big Hatteras, I was struck by how quiet the yacht was. Where was everyone else on this boat? Why had the girl been running up and down the dock? Couldn't the Blackwoods help? And Lorenzo's wife Catherine must be with him.... These musings were cut short as I joined the group and we were quickly ushered through the boat. The owner's suite was on the bow of the main level, but to my surprise we didn't head there but instead went down the stairs past the open laundry room door and down a narrow hall. The door at its end was open, and even though I was at the back, I could see the blood on the floor.

Greg sprang into action, looking for a pulse and assessing injures. Thomas pushed the shaken cook toward me with a grunt as he looked about him, trying to figure out what had happened. Steph turned white and excused herself, saying she was going to look in on Lorenzo's wife, Catherine.

"Good idea," we all seemed to say at once but at different times; actually, we had all forgotten about Catherine.

Realizing that calming down and questioning the young cook was the most helpful thing I could do for the moment, I took her by both shoulders and directed her back up the stairs to the galley, where I knew as cook she would be most comfortable. I sat her down, then went to pour us both a cup of coffee. Looking at her sitting there, pale and shaking, I decided that perhaps coffee wasn't enough, telling her to stay put I went in search of a blanket and some Kahlua to add to the coffee.

I retraced our path up to the main salon and grabbed a bottle off the bar, then a blanket from the first guestroom I saw; as the bed was unmade I assumed it must be the Blackwoods. I returned and wrapped the cashmere throw around the girl's shoulders and gave her the Kahlua coffee.

After she had had a few sips with shaking hands and had started to regain some composure, I gently started to ask her questions.

"Nancy…I'm Janeva; you were so kind to my daughter Katie when we here for dinner last night. I'm sorry—I don't know you last name?"

"Nancy… Nancy Fern."

"Where are you from, Nancy?"

"Pensacola, Mississippi."

"So that explains your pretty accent, but wow, you are a long way from home," I replied soothingly. "Is your family there?"

This worked, and she told me about her mother who had raised her and her brother and her cat, the town and many other details of her life before she had joined this crew.

"How old are you?" I finally managed to inquire as she took a sip of her coffee.

"I just turned 21 last month."

"Have you worked on the Atlantis for long?" I asked, knowing that if I kept her talking, soon she would relax and the whole story would probably come pouring out.

"Almost two years.... I really wanted to work on a cruise ship." She paused. "My friend Mary and me... well, by the time we had saved up enough money waitressing to get us to Fort Lauderdale, all the cruise boats had left. Apparently the Caribbean season was done," she sighed, "so I joined this boat as it had just come out of a refit."

"Where are the rest of the crew?" I ventured to ask.

"I don't know... they have disappeared! I looked and looked for Carl and Sandy, I searched the boat. Oh God, what could have happened to them?" she cried, and started to sob again.

Amazed, and growing concerned, I asked, "And

what about Mrs. Moretti—Catherine—and the Blackwoods?"

Through sobs she said, "Mrs. Moretti is in bed asleep, she usually sleeps until 11 am."

"And the Blackwoods?" I persisted.

"I don't know, they are not in their room,... I looked for them before I found you."

"Not in their room?" I repeated, mystified.

"They had a big fight after the party last night... ; I think that's why Mrs. Moretti got her headache and went to bed even earlier than usual."

Unfortunately, Thomas walked into the room just then, and I had no chance to ask Nancy anything about the big fight.

Thomas, looking grim, only shook his head. "What now?" I asked, feeling a growing sense of unreality.

"I'm going to the bridge to use their radio... it should have better range than ours," he said quietly, and turned to leave.

"Cell phone?"

"Hmph. Coverage here sucks but maybe they have a satellite phone," he said, and he left.

Something was definitely very wrong. Thomas is usually not so cryptic. Determined now to find out what was going on, I topped up Nancy's coffee and followed him. When I caught up with him, Thomas was standing on the bridge talking on the VHF radio, "Mayday, Mayday, Mayday.... We require immediate assistance; a man has been stabbed." I stopped, stunned... did he say stabbed?

The conversation continued between Thomas and the Canadian Coast Guard, Thomas describing our location, the vessel name, the nature of the wound, and finally current weather conditions.

The Coast Guard said that they would get a boat to us quickly, in fact they had just dispatched a fast inflatable from Sechelt and were checking into weather conditions to see if they could get a helicopter to us. Next they wanted an update on Lorenzo's condition, so Thomas sent me down to find out.

With a deep foreboding, I ran down the curved stairway leading from the bridge to the main level, then through the galley and down the next stairway to the hallway leading to Lorenzo's office. Here I stopped running, time seemed to slow down as I walked the last ten feet of the hallway. I could smell the blood even before I looked in the office doorway. There was Lorenzo, lying on his back in a pool of dark blood with a knife sticking out of his chest. I staggered and fell back against the doorway as the implications of what I was seeing registered. Greg, who had tried unsuccessfully to revive Lorenzo, was now putting various instruments back in his medical bag as he carefully avoided touching the knife or moving Lorenzo. Greg looked up at me, then jumped to his feet, grabbing my arm to steady me.

"Thomas, uh, Thomas asked me to come down and see how Lorenzo was," I stammered.

"He is deceased. I would say from his current state that he succumbed to the stabbing wound late last night. This is a matter for the police now." Greg took me by the arm and gently directed me out the doorway. "Go tell Thomas so he can alert the authorities."

"What are you going to do?" I asked. Greg's matter-of-fact, professional voice had cleared my head.

"I found the door key in Lorenzo's hand so I'm going to lock the door. We can't have anyone tampering with the evidence," he replied.

It was with a heavy heart that I returned to tell Thomas that Lorenzo was dead. At this news the Coast Guard transferred Thomas to the RCMP.

"RCMP?" I mouthed in a question.

"The Royal Canadian Mounted Police," he replied as he waited for them to come on the radio.

"Mounted Police???"

He shrugged, looking as bewildered as I felt. Shouldn't we be talking to the provincial police? Mounted—did they plan on riding horses to come to our aid? I know we are way out in the forest and the weather is getting worse fast, but really…horses?

Just then a wave of rain and wind slammed into the boat. Looking around, I realized that during the time I had been in the lowest level of this huge yacht, what had been a foggy but still and peaceful morning had turned into a storm with high winds and fierce sideways-blowing rain and… a murdered man!!!

I looked away from the window and the growing storm outside and met Thomas's eyes. "KATIE!" I turned and ran off the boat with Thomas close behind. Reaching our boat, I saw that the wind and waves were so strong it was actually heeling over at the dock. Calling Katie's name even before we boarded, I rushed below and collapsed, soaked from the rain and in tears of relief as Katie looked up at us with a confused look on her face.

"What's wrong?" she inquired looking from one of us to the other. We were a sight to see, having run down the dock through the pelting rain. Thomas, relieved to find his daughter safe and apparently oblivious to the storm, turned to go back outside.

"Where are you going?

"To check the lines again, then get back on the radio."

"At least change into dry clothes and put your foul weather gear on first."

Looking down at his wet jeans as if noticing them for the first time, he shivered and moved past us to our cabin to change. Soon he handed me a bundle of soaking clothes to hang in the head (bathroom) to dry.

"Lock this door behind me and don't leave the boat," Thomas said, with a meaningful look in my direction.

I shivered, both from the cold and wet and from the realization that there was a murderer in our midst.

Then I changed my clothes, cranked the heat up on
the boat, and sat down at the table with a steaming
cup of tea. Watching the steam rise from the cup, I
tried to console myself that the murderer would
have left this morning at slack tide. How long ago
was that, I wondered as I consulted my watch. It
was only 10:45 am! All this had happened in only
one hour!

Chapter Five

Council of War

Knock, knock, knock. "It's me, let me in," came Thomas's voice from outside the companionway hatch. I stood up to let him in and received a full face of wind and rain as a thank you.

"Get your coat, Janeva; we're going over to the Writemans' boat to talk about what's happened."

"What about the body? Shouldn't you stay with it, in case someone tampers with the evidence?" I asked.

"You watch to many TV shows," Thomas replied with a eye roll, but then conceded, "I checked the door and it's locked and solid. I asked Nancy and she said that Lorenzo had the only key, but as a precaution I broke into the key box and took all the keys off the boat, then I locked all the outside doors. I don't want those two missing crew members or anyone else on that boat until the RCMP arrive," he added, lifting a small duffel bag. "Nancy is sitting with Catherine, and she is to call me on the walkie talkie if anyone tries to get on that yacht or anything else happens."

"Oh God, what will you do if the murdering crew members DO show up?" I asked, alarmed.

"First of all I'm sure they are long gone—left with the morning slack tide. If not, I will deal with them when and if it they show up. Now, come on!"

"I'm coming too!" announced Katie. She had finished her movie and was bored, plus she had no intention of missing out on what was clearly an unusual and interesting situation.

Thomas immediately said "No."

Katie held her ground and glared back at him defiantly.

Being the peacemaker of the family, I rationally pointed out that "I would rather have her with us, and I think she should know what's going on."

Thomas turned his glare to me; I glared back.

It was one of those special family moments, with everyone glaring at each other. As Katie and I turned from Thomas to glare at each other, the corners of my mouth started to twitch, then smile. It was contagious and soon we were both laughing, with Thomas looking at us, mystified.

"Are you guys coming?" came the cry from Steph and Greg's cabin cruiser tied up in front of us on the dock.

"On our way!" replied Thomas and gestured for us all to get out of the boat, Katie included.

The Writemans' salon had two white-leather settees or sofas at arranged in an L shape, with a coffee table in front of the "L" on the port (left) side. The floor was a dark wood and the large windows were covered with white blinds. The whole effect was of a very elegant and calm space, very much like the calm and collected Writemans.

Katie and I took our seats on the long settee across from Stephanie and Greg, who were already seated drinking coffee. Thomas who came in last smiled and headed directly for the corner of the "L" and put up his feet. We had all taken our shoes off at the door, as is our custom when boating in the rain. Looking especially pleased and relaxed in his favorite position, with his arms on the back of the couch, Thomas grinned. Then, as he looked around, his expression changed.

"Well, we have landed ourselves in quite the mess.... We can't leave now until the police—pardon me, the RCMP—arrive, so we might as well piece together what we know, while we wait."

"What happened? Why can't we leave? What was the lady screaming about?" demanded Katie.

We all looked at her, startled, and realized that she had no idea of the past hour's events. We quickly filled her in, leaving out any graphic details.

"Oh, goody," she exclaimed. "I've always wanted to have a council of war." Again we all looked at her, surprised. This was not the response we expected from an 11-year old-girl upon hearing that a man she had met, though briefly, the night before had just been murdered less than 50 feet away.

Taking charge, Thomas said, "Let's start this, um... council of war, then," winking at Katie, "in a logical manner. First we should compare what we know."

"Is the murderer still here?" asked Katie with some alarm, as the import of what she had just learned registered.

"No, sweetie, it looks like everyone but us, Mrs. Moretti, and that girl left this morning to catch the slack tide. So we are safe, I'm sure; the murderer is long gone."

"Oh... good—but we are going to try and figure out who it was for the police?"

We all smiled back at her indulgently. The Writemans hadn't been able to have children and absolutely adored Katie, having known her since she was born and having spent many holidays with us. I stood up and went to the counter.

"Steph, do you have a notepad and a pen?... No, on second thought a pencil, if you have one, would be better. We have lots on our boat for Katie's homework, but it's so miserable outside."

At that we all turned to look outside. It appeared that the wind and rain were building.

"Here you go." Steph handed me the requested notebook and pencil.

"Ok, let's start with a timeline. What time did that

girl come screaming for help?" said Thomas,
looking at us as if we were his board members.

"It was before the 9:54 am slack tide…hmmm,"
Greg hesitated, lost in recollection. "Yes, about 9:10
am," he finally pronounced.

"Good, then we followed the girl to—" Thomas
continued.

"Nancy, Nancy Fair... no, Farie.... Fern! That's it," I
interrupted Thomas.

"That's what?" growled Thomas, looking annoyed.

"Her name, the girl, it's Nancy Fern," I replied,
smiling and writing it down, not the least bit
perturbed by Thomas's glare.

I relayed what Nancy had told me, making notes as
I went. Next it was Steph's turn to give us
Catherine's story.

"Believe it or not she was asleep when I found her,"
she shuddered. "I was surprised that anyone could
sleep through all the commotion, but she had taken
sleeping pills and had ear plugs in, plus I gather she
is used to the staff and other guests walking around
and usually sleeps late."

"So she knew nothing of her husband's death?" I
asked.

"No" was the quiet answer.

"Did you tell her?" I finally had the courage to ask
after a long pause.

"Well, sort of." She paused again. "I told her that
there had been an accident and that Lorenzo, her

husband, had been badly hurt." An even longer pause followed.

"And, well, it didn't seem to phase her!" Steph looked around at all of us with a very perplexed look, and then continued with her story. It went as follows:

"Believe it or not, she asked—no, asked isn't the right word—she demanded to see John."

"John? John Blackwood?" I clarified.

"Yes, John Blackwood," continued Stephanie. "Then, when I said I didn't know, she, Catherine, yelled at me, 'Where is he? I need him!'" Steph shook her head as she relived the conversation. "'Okay, okay,' I answered Catherine, 'I will go and look for him.' So I left her and went in search of the Blackwoods' cabin. It wasn't hard to find as they were the only guests on the yacht, but it was empty! I looked in the closets, drawers, head—everything was gone, and they had left! Believe me, I wasn't keen on going back to Catherine with that news. So I went down to find one of you to help me, but Janeva was in deep conversation with the young cook, Greg was still with Lorenzo and he told me about his death, Thomas, I didn't know where you were, and as I went back up to the main deck to start looking for you, I heard Catherine calling for John over and over again, so I took a deep breath and went into her cabin. She was propped up on the pillows in her bed, using all of them, including Lorenzo's. I realized then that I had to tell her, so taking a deep breath I just straight out told her that her husband was dead and John and Stella had left and that I didn't know where or when but all their stuff was missing.

"Catherine started to cry, a quiet, sad cry, and grabbed her legs and rolled up into a ball. I didn't know what to do and was about to go for Greg, knowing he would know, when she quietly asked me for a glass of water. I went to the galley and found a bottle of water. It was only after I had handed it to her and she had spun the top off and taken a big drink that I realized she had taken more sleeping pills. Fortunately for me, Greg arrived at Catherine's doorway a minute later," she continued with a faint smile. "He checked her pulse and other vitals, concluding that she had only taken two and was just going to have to sleep it off." Steph then took a deep breath herself and looked much better, as if getting her story out of the way had taken a load off her.

Thomas told us about the calls with the Canadian Coast Guard and police. Then it was Greg's turn. His account was rather graphic though fortunately very medical; the technical terminology made it difficult for me to follow, much less Katie. I really didn't want her visualizing the gruesome murder. After several attempts to spell complicated medical words I handed the notepad over to Steph.

"Can you take over? I'm a terrible speller even with normal words, plus doctor-speak is way out of my league," I said, smiling apologetically. "Plus, you are the writer here, so why am I doing this anyway?" I teased, as I handed the pad and pencil to

Steph.

"And I'm hungry," announced Katie, who was always hungry these days and growing like a weed. She was already only a few inches shorter than me.

"No need to go back to your boat, there is plenty of food in ours. We could all use a snack," Steph replied with a smile.

As Katie and I stood to walk the few feet to the galley I happen to look out in time to see Trent's boat pass us, going back to the dock.

"What's he doing back? I guess we better go and grab some lines; we know his wife isn't one for jumping off the boat."

"Especially in the rain," Greg added, laughing.

"We got it; you girls stay here and work on lunch," Thomas said as he and Greg grabbed their rain gear and headed out to help the returning boats dock.

After some rummaging around in the fridge, Steph, Katie, and I were able to pull together a great lunch of cheese quesadillas, veggies and dip, and some potato chips that Katie found in the snack cupboard and used her considerable talent to convince us were exactly what we needed to cheer us up.

Thomas and Greg returned.

"Finally you're back; what took you so long?" Katie demanded of her father and Greg. Of course the only reason that she cared was because I, her mother, wouldn't let her have any of the potato chips until they returned, knowing full well that once we started to eat them we couldn't stop.

"You won't believe it," Thomas hesitated, waiting to get our attention. Once he had it, he continued, "Well, we found out where John and Stella Blackwood disappeared to—" he paused here, making sure he had all our attention.

When I finally gave in and cried "Where?" Thomas happily continued on : "They were on Trent's boat. And it wasn't just Trent's boat that came in! All the boats are back! Apparently a tree fell in the wind storm and has blocked the Malibu Rapids."

"What... we're trapped here?!" I exclaimed.

Greg, ever the calm voice of reason, chimed in: "Well, they think that the tree would probably get washed out with the current at high tide later today, so we should be able to leave this afternoon at slack tide."

"BUT UNTIL THEN WE ARE STUCK HERE WITH A MURDERER!" I cried. This accurate statement had the effect of a full stop as the reality of it registered with everyone, and we all stared at each other in horror.

"We didn't tell them about Lorenzo!" Thomas exclaimed, breaking the silence.

We all looked at each other, grim-faced.

"Oh God," I groaned. "I was kind of okay staying here with a corpse until the police or Coast Guard arrived because I was 100 percent sure the killer had fled BUT not so much now that everyone is back and we are stuck here with them."

"You're getting yourself all worked up," scolded Thomas, who was always in control.

"Of course I am, and for good reason. What about Katie? We can't just sit here! We have to do something!" I retorted.

"Okay, what do you suggest we do?"

"For starters, we need to find out what's happening on that boat, now that all the suspects are back."

"What makes you think the murderer is a Yacht Club member? What about the missing crew? Or the other boats that were anchored out or at the dock last night?"

"Oh, I hate it when you are right!" I snarled. "Well, I don't think it was a random act, do you?"

"No, it's pretty clear that it was someone he knew. How else could they have gotten on the boat and been with him in his office?"

"Why do you say that?" Steph inquired.

We all turned to look at her. We had been so involved in the verbal debate we had forgotten she was there.

"Right—you didn't see the body! He was wearing the same clothes he had on that night at dinner, and had a half-drunk glass of scotch on his desk," Greg replied.

"Pure speculation: we need facts!" interjected Thomas. "I vote we go back and see what we can find out."

Nodding his agreement, Greg said, "Janeva is right, I'm sure Catherine is in hysterics by now."

"No way, I'm not going anywhere near that boat," pronounced Steph.

"Will you hang out with Katie, then?" I asked.

"Love to! Katie, let's play that board game you were telling me about."

"YES!" came Katie's immediate reply.

Leaving Katie and Steph safely locked in the boat, happily debating the merits of different board games, the rest of us put our wet rain gear back on and headed over to the scene of the crime on the yacht Atlantis.

Just before boarding, Thomas stopped us.

"Good: the Blackwoods are both still at Trent's boat!... We need a plan," he said as he looked at me.

"Fine," I grumbled, "what do you have in mind?"

"We need to play to our strengths here. I'll go up to the bridge and get back on the radio, let the police and Coast Guard know about the tree, and find out when they think they can get here.

"Greg, you should check on the body, make sure it's secure... and that no one has disturbed it. Janeva, check on Catherine and Nancy the cook. I expect we will be seeing Trent, Wiffy, John, and Stella soon enough, so let's try and detain them in the salon until the police arrive."

"Right; better to observe them and see who acts guilty!" I exclaimed. "Greg, here—take my phone and get some photos of the crime scene," I added.

"Janeva, this isn't a TV show, this is REAL," growled Thomas. "Try to control yourself; we could be in real danger."

"Okay, okay; what do you want me to do?" I asked.

"Look around, see if you can find out what happened to the two other crew members. They have to be somewhere, and we didn't see them on Trent's boat."

A half hour later found us sitting on the settee in the lavish main salon of the Atlantis.

"Well," I broke the silence, "what did the Coast Guard and police say?"

"Nothing... in short, we are trapped here until the storm—well, fog in particular—clears up, and/or that tree moves. Did you find any sign of the missing crew, and how are Catherine and the cook?"

"No sign of the two missing crew. I checked the cabin, and their uniforms, toiletries, etc. are still there. I did a quick search of the boat and didn't see anything else amiss," I replied. "Catherine is still sleeping and I was able to calm Nancy down by ordering up a huge lunch." Looking around, I mused, "I know we've already eaten, but she needed something to do, and anyway I'm sure Trent's group will be happy to have lunch." I paused for breath. "As requested, I also asked her about the missing crew. Apparently Carl, the first mate, was a diesel mechanic by trade and one of his jobs was to keep the boat running. He also drove the boat when Lorenzo got bored or was entertaining, did any repairs, and did all the other maintenance to keep the boat in tip-top shape."

"What about the body?" Thomas asked.

Greg held up a key: "Just as I left it."

"Are we sure that John or Stella don't have a key?" Thomas asked, looking worried.

"Nancy said... when I asked her if she had seen anyone going into Lorenzo's office, what was most interesting is that she said it's always locked, only Lorenzo had keys," I replied.

"Oh, it sounds like we are about to have company," Greg interrupted, hearing voices and standing up to look outside on the dock.

John and Stella Blackwood were walking alongside, chatting amiably with Trent and his wife.

"What are we going to say to them?" I asked.

Thomas steepled his fingers, looking thoughtful.

"Here is what we are going to do. Janeva, you head off the women, and find out why John and Stella left. We know Trent was planning to leave this morning, but there was no mention of John and Stella going with them at dinner last night. Distract them with the missing crew, and if asked if you have seen Lorenzo, say he is sick or missing if they press you. Watch their faces, look for discomfort; one of them might be our killer."

Chapter Six

The Call

From a telephone transcript acquired by Janeva in a later book, she felt it important and appropriate to add here

Looking at his watch as he typed furiously on his laptop, Max thought Why does everything always happen at the last minute? I'm about to board, and now this!

Grabbing his iPhone and dialing, he demanded into the device, "…Where are you?!"

"Princess Louisa," came the faint voice.

"Why are you still there?" growled Max.

"A storm,… never mind, I can barely hear you, we have a bad connection…."

"Did you get it, in the shoe?" snapped Max.

"Yes."

"You need to distance yourself from that shoe until the shoe unwittingly transports the code to its destination, so get out of there, NOW! " Max said, and ended the conversation.

Max put down his iPhone. As he sat waiting for his plane to be ready for him to board, his mind wandered. I'm sick of traveling, it used to be fun but now I find it tedious, man I miss the old days when I first founded the company. It was fun back then, a small, creative, hardworking team. That was 13 years ago; now we're almost 60,000 people worldwide. We have become self-perpetuating, we need to grow to expand, make more money, or the shareholders revolt.

Finally boarded and in his favorite seat, Max sat staring blankly at the tarmac

His iPhone chimed, bringing him out of his reverie. Only a text. He would reply on the plane. Max picked up his bag and headed to his flight.

Smiling, Max accepted a drink from the flight attendant.

His thoughts again ran to the future of the company. It was his life, and had consumed him. I need that product, architecture and code! he mused. And before they announce their new product! He slammed his empty glass down on his armrest so hard that some ice flew out. This is our space. We can't have that company beating us at our own game! We need to know exactly how they are building it and rush our version to market before them: it will crush them.

"Would you like another one?" asked the flight attendant in a soft Southern voice.

Scowling, he held up his glass for her to take. "Damn-it, yes," he replied as he looked at her appreciatively. He had no family. True, there was always a string of girlfriends who were more than happy to join him on his private plane and stay in luxury hotels around the world as he checked on his business assets. But even they were getting boring. Most had so little of value to talk about, and the interesting ones had lives and careers that they weren't willing to give up to join him in his gypsy lifestyle.

Chapter Seven

"Hurry up!"

I cornered Stella as soon as she stepped into the
main salon where I had been sitting with Thomas
and Greg just moments before. Thomas and Greg
got up to intercept Trent and John Blackwood on
the back deck.

"Where is, is...Wiffy?" I asked Stella; I still
struggled with Trent's wife's name. "I'm sorry I
don't remember her real or full name?"

Stella laughed, a strange sound in the
circumstances. But her obvious ease boded well for
her innocence.

"I doubt you were ever told it," she replied, "I
wasn't." She giggled. "Wiffy finds Catherine to be a
bit over the top, if you know what I mean?" she
leaned in conspiratorially. "You may not have

noticed, but Catherine is a bit of a princess and Wiffy finds it just too much to bear so she avoids coming over here."

Just then John came in with their travel bags, nodded at me in greeting, and proceeded toward their cabin to drop them off.

As Stella watched him, I felt her mood change. She had been in a cheerful, calm mood, but as her husband walked past her smile faded and her face fell and went pale. I looked at her with concern.

"Are you okay?" I asked.

She made a visible effort to regain her composure and then broke into tears.

I was astonished. Was this a confession so quickly? I wondered. Not really knowing what to do, I put an arm around her shoulders and made soft comforting noises.

After a time she asked for a drink. I was more than happy to provide her with one, not knowing what else to do.

I handed her a gin and tonic, sat down beside her, and said nothing. Actually I was wracking my brain about what to say. I kept coming up with this and that and then rejecting the ideas just as quickly. But not saying anything must have been the right approach because as Stella sipped her G and T she started to talk so quietly that I had to move in to hear her.

"I thought that his infatuation with Catherine was

finally over.... I thought that when he woke me this morning demanding that we pack and leave, that just maybe he had finally seen through her, or they had had a fight and it was over," she sniffed, and then put her head in her arms on the sofa pillows of the settee and started to cry softly again.

"What happened?" I asked. I could tell by her pleading look that she wanted to tell me but didn't know how. "Start at the beginning," I suggested gently.

Stella's story went as follows:

> "Stella, Stella, get up!" John whispered urgently as he shook his wife Stella awake from a deep sleep.
>
> "What... why? It's only 8 in the morning," she replied sleepily, as she rolled over.
>
> "I mean it: get up now! We have to go."
>
> Realizing by the tone of his voice that her husband meant it, she sat up and looked at him quizzically. "Go where?"
>
> "I'll explain later. Just get out of bed and get dressed," John said, as he threw a pair of jeans and a T-shirt at her and then started packing their clothes into their suitcases haphazardly.

"The next thing I knew, we were on the Braise-Bottoms' boat, leaving," Stella concluded.

"Do you know why John was in such a rush to leave, Stella?" I inquired gently.

"Oh, he said something about needing to get back to

work, and that's true, we have a flight booked out of Vancouver tomorrow," Stella said with a shrug. "When you live with John you get used to stuff like that," she finished with a small smile.

We looked up as Thomas walked into the salon, followed by Greg, John, and Trent.

"The Coast Guard and RCMP are here," announced Thomas.

"How did they get here so quickly?" I asked.

"Take a look outside." Thomas gestured to the window.

I did, and was astounded to see that a massive 88-foot Type 400 AP1 Coast Guard Hovercraft had pulled up and was rafting to the Atlantis.

"They cleared the tree across the rapids on their way in," Thomas said, answering my unasked question. He had only just stopped speaking as the official-looking group walked in.

"I am Inspector Stanley, and this is... " the head of the group said, then continued to introduce the rest of RCMP and Coast Guard, but I tuned out, alarmed by Catherine's arrival in the room. Her face was white, she was swaying, and looked terrified. I started toward her, unnoticed, since Thomas and the rest were deep in conversation with the police and the Coast Guard. I made it to Catherine just in time to catch her as she collapsed, and eased her into a nearby chair.

"Catherine! What's wrong?" Even as the words left

my mouth I wished I could swallow them back. Of course I knew what was wrong—her husband had just been brutally murdered! Quick thinking has never been my strength; I ponder and analyze things, but that approach was not helping me now. So, seeing that Stella needed another drink, I did the logical thing and told Catherine that what she needed right now was a gin and tonic. Clearly that was the last thing she needed, but it was the best I could come up with.

Thomas, Greg, John, and Trent disappeared with the official-looking group of inspectors, to view the body, aka crime scene, leaving me with the women, so I went to make them two strong gin and tonics. To my relief, both women readily accepted the drinks. At first I was surprised that we were left alone but as I handed the around the G and Ts, I noticed that there were police stationed on the deck of the boat, guarding the exits, and others on the dock. I guess I shouldn't have been so surprised it was a murder, and this wasn't an area where murders happened frequently. Plus that huge hovercraft could bring a whole regiment on it.

~~~~~~~~~~~~~~~~

After surveying the body, Inspector Stanley determined that the yacht was indeed a crime scene. This turned out to be unfortunate for everyone who had hopes of leaving. We were ordered to gather and wait in the salon, while RCMP officers were dispatched to collect Steph and Katie and search all our boats.

"Mom!" Looking uncharacteristically scared and

confused, Katie dropped Steph's hand and ran into my arms. "What? Why? Um... "

"It's okay, honey, the policemen are just doing their jobs," I said, hugging her. Even though the situation was appalling, I was enjoying hugging Katie and I felt better having her close, especially as the RCMP were acting like the murderer was one of us! And on consideration, I guessed that—with the rapids being blocked and there being no other way in or out of the area—the murderer was sure to still be in the area.

"We were in the middle of our board game," whined Katie. "Why did we have to leave and what are they looking for?"

At this point Thomas arrived to stand beside us. "They are interviewing everyone." I looked up at him, surprised. I hadn't realized he was being interviewed. A police officer appeared behind him. Looking at me, he asked politely,

"Are you Thomas's wife?"

"Yes, I'm Janeva," I replied.

"Is this your daughter?"

"Yes, this is Katie," I replied.

"She will need to be interviewed also," he replied.

At this point Katie broke into tears.

"We can't have you swapping stories," the officer said. Pointing at Katie he added, "You are next, young lady." At this Katie and I looked at him in alarm

"I'm not comfortable with my 11-year-old daughter being interrogated," Thomas stated angrily.

Moving his hands with his palms outstretched in a calming manner, the officer continued, "Let me finish. As you have already been interviewed, you may go with her if you promise not to speak, help, or interrupt." Thomas nodded to agree, and Katie clung even tighter to me, if that was possible.

"Honey, you must go, don't worry, your Dad will be right beside you." This registered with Katie. She let me go and transferred her affection to Thomas, her new champion.

They weren't gone long as Katie had no information for them, having stayed on our boat or the Writemans'. Then it was my turn. I didn't get off so quickly, and it felt like hours of questioning; the officer must have asked each question ten different ways. I was exhausted and emotionally drained when I finally returned to our boat several hours later.

The boat was a disaster. The officers had clearly searched it: books, clothes, charts, and DVDs were scattered throughout the boat. Turning, I went in search of Thomas and Katie, who were exactly where I expected them to be: curled up on the settee of the Writemans' boat.

"Here, you look like you need this," Steph said as she handed me a gin martini.

"Thank you, this is exactly what I need." Gratefully

taking a big sip of the relaxing beverage, I asked, "Did they trash your boat also?"

"Yes, Greg and I got it put back together fairly quickly once we started. Do you want me to help you with your boat?"

"Thank you, but I'll rally my troops off your settee and we will get it done."

"Are they looking for the murder weapon?" Katie asked.

"Must be. When I left Lorenzo and Catherine's boat the Coast Guard were scuba diving under the boat and dock," I replied.

"The RCMP sent a team up the waterfall path, too," added Greg. "They must be looking for those missing crew members.

"Oh that's good, I'm sure they are the murderers," Steph said. "I hope they catch them so we can leave."

"Hear, hear!" Thomas said. "I've had it with this place. I hope we will be free to go after the RCMP have finished interviewing everyone and collecting our names, addresses, phone numbers, and travel plans."

"I hope so, too," Steph said with feeling.

"They warned us if they weren't able to contact us they would have us detained at U.S. Customs. It appears that the police are pretty sure that the two missing crew were the guilty party," Greg added.

"I wonder why they killed him?" Katie asked.

"That's and excellent question, honey. We will probably never know.... Who knows what Lorenzo and Catherine were like to work for, or what secrets were festering on that yacht? I'm sure the Canadian police will figure it all out and we will read about it in the paper soon," I replied.

Thomas, Greg, Trent, and John had all petitioned the RCMP and Coast Guard with our need and desire to leave. No one wanted to spend another night at Princess Louisa and we needed to start making our way home. Summer was over, along with our holidays, and I still had some back-to-school shopping to do for Katie. Fortunately for us, the police agreed, feeling that they had all the information they needed for the time being. They took possession of the Atlantis, sending Catherine back to the States on Trent's boat, and informed us all that we still had to go through Customs, so if they had additional questions or had found anything to discredit our statements, we would be detained in Vancouver. The moment we deemed the current slake enough for us to motor through the rapids, we happily joined the line of boats heading out of Princess Louisa.

It was wonderful to be free of the fog; though it was still rainy, we at least had better visibility than before. In tandem with Greg and Steph, we headed for home.

Chapter Eight

Homeward Bound

Leaving Princess Louisa behind us, we turned to see the Malibu Rapids fade away in the distance.

"Finally, we are homeward bound," I said.

"What a way to end the summer," Thomas said, turning to look forward at the horizon and blue sky.

"Not what you had in mind?" I asked.

"No, I planned on sun and relaxation, and now that we have to go home. Just look at the weather…it's spooky that just as we're finally leaving Princess Louisa, it's all sun and blue sky."

"Well, we were pushing the season. This is Canada and fall starts early here," I teased.

"Yeah, Dad, the further north you go the colder it

gets."

"Humph. Okay, I suppose we can't complain about the weather—but a murder?"

"At least it was exciting," Katie contributed.

"True, but I don't go boating for excitement," grumped Thomas in reply.

Katie turned her head and looked at him inquiringly, while I tried to stifle a giggle.

"To relax and enjoy nature." Thomas threw the boat cloth at her that he had been using to wipe the dew off of the seats and life lines. "Stop teasing me and wipe down the windows so I can see better."

"After I do the windows, can I go down below and watch a movie?" Katie asked.

"You are just trying to get out of sight so we don't give you any more boat jobs," I replied, smiling. "Don't look so surprised that I'm on to you. I was young once, too, you know. Here is the deal: after you've finished wiping down the windows you need to read for an hour; then you can watch your movie. It's going to be a long trip home."

Glaring at me, Katie countered, "What are you going to do?"

"You had better drop the attitude, young lady, or I won't turn on the inverter that powers your DVD player and TV."

Giving me a big bright smile, Katie went instantly from sulky to cheerful in the way that only a pre-teen can.

"I'm going to finish wiping down the table and seats, then I'm going to make some bread. If that meets with your approval?" I said.

"Can you make cookies or brownies instead?" Katie asked with optimism.

"No, but you can," I replied.

"Okay," came her enthusiastic answer.

"But you have to make them by yourself and do all the cleanup."

"Humph... Dad, why don't you make a 3D printer that can make chocolate chip cookies or brownies?"

"Ha ha, like the food replicator on Star Trek," Thomas laughed. His company makes commercial 3D printers.

"Why not?" inquired Katie.

"Maybe someday. But our 3D printers work with an additive process, where an object is created by laying down successive layers of material.

"What is 3D printing exactly?" Katie asked, clearly confused. "3D printing is a process of making three-dimensional solid objects from a digital model. An example for you might be making a clay pinch pot. I know you like to make things with clay, correct?"

"Yes, I made Mom a pinch pot last year and she keeps her favorite earrings in it."

"Right. First, let's say you drew out a detailed picture of the exact pot you wanted. Our products are made from digital drawings or complex computer code, ... Then you would make your pinch pot by taking a ball of clay, working with it until you could stick your thumbs in the middle and pull up the sides to make a bowl." Here Thomas looked at Katie for her nod of both agreement and that she was still listening and following.

"That is called a subtractive process in traditional manufacturing techniques, which mostly rely on the removal of material by drilling, cutting, or in the case of a pinch pot using your thumbs and a wheel to pull at the clay and make your shape.

"Our 3D printing machines make products by building them up instead—more like making a coil pot. For a coil pot you roll the clay between your hands until you make long coils, then you stack the coils one on top of the other until you have made the shape of a bowl. That's exactly what our 3D printing machines do, but we make plastic and metal components. We're a long way from being able to crack eggs, mix in liquids and flour and other dry ingredients, then cook them. That said, we just incorporated phase-change memory chips into our machines, and who knows where that might lead in the future?"

"What is phase-change memory?" I asked, intrigued. I had never heard of it before.

"Phase-change memory is a type of non-volatile random-access memory that—"

"I'm leaving now," interrupted Katie as she disappeared down into the boat, her window wiping completed.

Laughing, I said, "Either she has gone to make a pinch pot, watch a movie, or both. Now tell me about this memory, and why is it important?"

"Well, phase-change memory chips are both faster and more durable than traditional flash memory. What's really exciting is it can retain information even when the power is switched off."

"How does it do that?"

"Phase-change memory chips rely on a glass-like material called chalcogenides." Noting my confused expression, he continued, "Chalcogenides is, as I said, a glass-like material typically made of a mixture of germanium, antimony, and tellurium."

"Okay, and why is this special glass so great?"

"This glass can switch between two states: crystalline and amorphous. The amorphous state is a disorderly state; think of the amorphous state being binary code '0,' compared to a crystalline or orderly state with a binary number '1'. Chalcogenides can do this switch very quickly when an electrical current causes one of the electrodes on either side of the chalcogenides to heat up, thus causing the chalcogenides to melt to an amorphous or disorderly state, and as it cools again if forms a crystalline structure or orderly state."

"That's very cool, but why is it better than traditional flash memory?" I asked, trying to visualize this glass-like structure changing from a solid to liquid form quickly, still unclear how that holds memory.

"Writing to individual flash-memory cells involves erasing the entire region of neighboring cells first. This is not necessary with phase-change memory, which makes it much faster. In fact, some prototype phase-change memory devices can store and retrieve data a hundred times faster than flash memory."

Deciding that the conversation was getting a bit technical, I asked, "So how does this new memory chip help your 3D printing machines?"

"Our machines are currently controlled from a laptop or computer. What we're working on is a machine with the computer built in. It will have a menu, sort of like a vending machine or Katie's food replicator from Star Trek, but not for food. Think of a plumber or car mechanic. Instead of having a truck or shop full of inventory and having to wait and order parts, they would have our 3D printers with a menu of all the possible parts and print what they needed on site. A component or part can even be scanned or searched for and loaded up to be printed."

"That's a huge benefit to a company! What a savings. Not having to keep a huge inventory, and phase-change memory makes this possible?" I asked.

"That's right. It's because the phase-change memory combines both RAM and ROM memory, so when you turn off the machine you don't lose anything. Plus, as I already mentioned, it's much smaller, and faster."

"I can't wait to see it in action!" I exclaimed. "Can I have a demo when we get home?"

"Of course, I would love to show it to you," Thomas said smiling.

"Great! Well, until you build Katie and me our 3D printing food replicator, I'd better get to making that bread so it has time to rise," I said, and headed down to the galley to start making the dough.

Chapter Nine

Yacht Club Fundraiser

The Archipelago Yacht Club we belong to is a traditional colonial-style building on the waterfront. Inside it is very elegant with its wood-paneled walls, dark leather furniture, and large fireplaces, plus the club has one of the best views in town. If you are lucky enough to be a member or know a member, you can book your wedding or special event in this beautiful venue. Membership in this private club is very expensive and you have to be sponsored and interviewed first; then you go on a wait list, as the club membership is full, only opening up as older members die. Like most of our friends at the Yacht Club we are second- or third-generation members. My parents were members and signed me up at the young age of seven, the earliest age you can become a junior member, so I had a lot of seniority in the club and that was helpful in securing a good berth (docking space) for our boat. We had signed Katie up at seven, too, continuing the tradition of family membership.

I had met Thomas at the Yacht Club during sailboat racing season. Thomas was an avid yacht racer and his family's race boat had won the cup for several years. I also enjoy racing sailboats, though I chose the fun boat instead. The club has many members, like our family, who are passionate about boating but aren't rich. That said, there is still a large percentage of the membership who are very wealthy, people with private jets, super yachts, and "trust fund kids" whose family trusts pays them a monthly amount plus a lump sum at various milestones in their lives (we secretly call them "the lucky sperm club"). The Yacht Club hosts many charity events and fundraising dinners as it's a great way for those fortunate members to give back, plus many of them really enjoy organizing the events.

Tonight's fall fundraiser was the first of the season and a benefit for cancer research, a cause that was dear to my heart, as one of our Yacht Club friends had passed away from a brain tumor the previous year. As we entered the formal dining room, I heard my name called.

"Janeva, Thomas—how are you? Come over to our table and say hi to Catherine and Stella," John Blackwood commanded, as he intercepted us. We obediently went with him to the table. For my part I was surprised to see Stella and Catherine chatting amiably, especially after the revelations on the boat a few weeks before, when we'd all been docked at the Yacht Club outstation in Princess Louisa Inlet, British Columbia.

"Sit, sit!" said John, pulling out a chair for me beside Stella and waving Thomas to one next to his, across the table.

We sat down; to do anything else would not have been polite. After an awkward silence a general conversation started up about what everyone had done after leaving Princess Louisa three weeks earlier. This, too, was awkward because no one mentioned Lorenzo's murder. Realizing that the presentations were to begin soon and wanting to sit with our regular group of friends, including Greg and Stephanie, we started to make our excuses. That group had saved seats for us at a table at the back of the room, where those of us who don't have huge fortunes to give big donations are relegated.

"It was good to see you all again; the program is about to start, so we had best get to our seats," I said, standing to an approving nod from Thomas

"No, no; you mustn't go. We're short two people at our table and it would look bad to have a front table not full," Catherine pronounced emphatically, looking concerned.

Thomas and I exchanged looks. There were two empty seats besides the ones we had filled, and we really didn't feel comfortable sitting with this group.

As if on cue, Trent Braise-Bottom the Third and his

wife appeared, and with smiles all around took the remaining two seats.

This was getting stranger by the minute, and to my great dismay the MC got up to start the event, thus making escape impossible. We were now, by all standards of polite conduct, committed to spend the evening, at least the dinner and presentation part of the evening, at the Blackwoods' table. This in itself was an interesting thought as they were not actually members of the club. Regardless, we were stuck, and could only wave sadly to our friends, who sat toasting and laughing at us from the back of the room. To add insult to injury, the table we had been trapped at was at the very front of the room and its occupants were actually expected to bid on auction items... we neither wanted nor could afford to bid on items like a weekend via private jet to Disneyland or a weeklong stay at a member's vacation home on Mystic Island in five-star luxury.

We managed to survive the bidding part of the evening and were relieved when the dancing started. Or so we thought.

"Thomas," I whispered. "Ask Catherine to dance!"

"Why?" he inquired, looking very perplexed

"She is getting sloshed and just ordered her third bottle of wine!"

"So? Lots of people are getting drunk."

"Right, but the more she drinks, the more she leans on John, and Stella looks furious."

"It's too bad John is such a nice guy... anyone else would have sent her home."

"Thomas, please?"

"Oh, okay, but you owe me."

So off they went to dance. Fortunately for Thomas it wasn't a slow dance, and they ended up dancing in a group.

"What's going on?" asked Steph, coming to sit beside me at the now empty table. Trent and his wife, Wiffy, had left early, and John and Stella had gone to join the dancing circle.

Looking at the dancing group in dismay, I replied, "I sent Thomas to dance with Catherine as she was downing bottles of champagne like water, then flirting with John. Stella is fuming, so I hoped to diffuse the situation, but as you can see it didn't work very well."

We both looked up to see Thomas at the bar, happily talking to our friends, Catherine dirty dancing with John, and Stella desperate to get John's attention by dirty dancing with another Yacht Club member, who was looking very uncomfortable and confused, thus ruining her whole performance.

"I just can't see this ending well," I said to Steph with a shake of my head, "but I don't know how to derail this train wreck."

Laughing at my analogy she said, "We need to get Catherine in a taxi and send her home!"

"And how do you propose we do that?" I inquired.

"Hmmm, good point. First we need to get her off the dance floor." Steph paused, looking around.

"Right," I said following her gaze. "Thomas failed to keep her dancing—"

"Maybe we can get John to dance her outside to a taxi?" she suggested.

The dance ended and Catherine came back to the table to gulp her champagne down like water.

"Now what?" Steph mouthed.

I gave her a slight shrug of my shoulders, then turned to Catherine, who was sitting beside me, and asked her if she was sleeping on her boat tonight, as we were.

"No," she slurred, it coming out more like Noooth. "Iths still impounded in Canada by the police."

"Oh, right, but you're not driving?" I asked, anticipating the standard drunk response of "I'm fine."

"John is driving" was her response, much to my relief. But it was short-lived given her next words— "John has been so sweet and supportive since Lorenzo's death, he has helped with everything...," here she stopped to refill her glass.

"John and Stella have been staying with you this whole time?" I asked, taken by surprise. "What about your family?"

"I don't have any," she replied, looking very sad. Having no good response, I just patted her hand.

"Papa died a few years back," she continued morosely. "My mom died when I was very young, so I have no siblings, and we were unable to have children" she finished.

"Oh," was all I could manage.

"But John has been wonderful," she said, as tears ran down her perfectly made-up cheeks.

I gave her a hug and said I would find John and Stella to take her home.

"She has no one," I said to Steph later, as the evening wrapped up. "It's no wonder she is clinging so hard to John. I'm extrapolating here, but it sounds like she was doted on by both her father and Lorenzo and never really grew up."

"Well, that might explain her helpless and childish behavior."

"I'm tired; where has Thomas disappeared to?"

We found Thomas and Greg in the games room in the middle of a pool game. We sat and watched for a short time; then, realizing that they were going to be a while, we left them to their game and headed back to our respective boats.

"Where is Katie tonight?" Steph asked as we walked down the dock.

"At a sleepover with her BFF Alix; see you tomorrow."

"Brunch at 11 o'clock?"

"I'll definitely be there!" I replied, "I can't speak for Thomas, it depends on how long he spends playing pool," I added, laughing.

Chapter Ten

Brunch at the Club

Surprisingly, both Thomas and Greg were up in time for brunch. We had fun exchanging stories over eggs benny and lattes in the Yacht Club's casual downstairs restaurant. I didn't have much to relate as I had been trapped with Catherine for the night, but I was able to share her sad family history and we all expressed gratitude that John and Stella had chosen to stay with her; it must be very lonely to have no one.

"I do find it strange that Catherine doesn't seem to have any friends of her own," I expressed.

"I heard that Lorenzo was very domineering," said Kevin. Kevin is a good friend and one of our group.

Kevin always reminded me of Fred Flintstone, not in his appearance, as he is of normal height and build with thick blond hair and grey cynical eyes, but in his personality, which is huge. You always know where Kevin is. He has a loud, carrying voice and booming laugh and he has no "inside voice" or filter. If he thinks it, he says it. As you can imagine, this has caused offense to many club members and staff, but if you take the time to get to know him he has a heart of gold and is extremely generous. He will drop everything to help a friend.

"Really; how do you know that?" I inquired, not really needing an answer because Kevin always seemed to be the first to know anything that was happening at the club. How he came by his information was a mystery to me, but his gossip is always good and fairly accurate, and I was interested to learn more about Lorenzo's and Catherine's relationship because we seemed to have been pulled into her life through Lorenzo's murder.

"My sources are confidential," he replied, with a big billowing laugh. "I know you, Janeva: you really want to know more but don't want to ask me directly," he smirked.

"Okay, okay; you're right," I admitted. "What else do you know?"

"Well," he leaned across the table, "apparently Lorenzo didn't like Catherine to have friends; he liked to have her at his beck and call."

"What on earth did she do all day if she had no friends or family?" Steph asked, joining the conversation. Thomas and Greg, who claim to hate gossip, had moved over to the next table and were in a discussion of club politics with some other good friends. Personally, I don't see how talking about what the commodore said to rear commodore, and then analyzing an argument between the staff captain and the fleet captain at the last executive meeting, is any different from what we were doing!

Kevin continued: "She spent a lot of time with her dad, who had been very ill over the last few years. Catherine was a only child and his main caregiver, I gather, as his health deteriorated. They even set up a hospital-style bed and room for him in the house with a night nurse coming to sit with him so Catherine could have evenings and nights off to be with Lorenzo and attend functions with him."

"I admire her. It's very sweet that she nursed her dad, but she must have had some friends?" I persisted.

"I'm not kidding, her dad was just like Lorenzo; that's why he was the only one Catherine was allowed to spend time with," Kevin answered.

"So she was essentially held hostage between her father and husband, to look after them and not otherwise to go out of the house?" I asked incredulously.

"Well, she had to look the part, so she spent lots of time and money at the spa, hair salon, and gym, and I think she made friends of a sort there, but I don't know where those friends are now."

"I can't decide if she should be lonely and distraught or excited at the prospect of doing whatever she wants. This is probably the first time in her life she has ever been free," Steph said, with a shake of her head and a sigh.

"I don't know about that," replied Kevin. "She seems to have replaced Lorenzo and her dad, who passed away last year, with John and Stella."

With that we had to end this interesting chat as Thomas returned to the table, saying it was time to go and pick up Katie from her sleepover.

~~~~~~~~~~~~~~~~~~~

"Mom, you'll never guess what Alix and I found on the Internet," Katie announced excitedly as she jumped in the car, waving a piece of printed paper at me.

"I can't drive and read it at the same time, I'll look at it when we get home," I said.

Back at the house, I picked up the single sheet of computer printed-paper to read, becoming increasingly alarmed as I did so.

Aug. 31, 2011 - ABC NEWS
Foot Washes Ashore in Canada, the 11th Since 2007

Another human foot has washed ashore in British Columbia, keeping investigators on their toes in the case of 11 mysterious feet in running shoes that have appeared on area beaches since 2007.
   Eight feet have washed up around Vancouver, and three feet have come ashore in nearby Washington State since 2007, according to Stephen Fonseca of the British Columbia Coroner's Service. None of the

cases has been deemed suspicious.

Fonseca said that human remains can come apart naturally in a water environment, and with the high amount of marine activity, and many people involved in accidents in the water, it's likely that these are all unrelated cases. He also noted that there are many bridges over waterways in the area, and distraught people who may have jumped could also be a source of the body parts washing up on shore.

"Running shoes of today are more buoyant," he said, "and it's a very rational explanation that when the feet do disarticulate, through marine scavenging and decomposition, the shoe will bring the foot back up to the surface and it will float there until it reaches shoreline."

The Coroner's Service will try to build a profile of the person to whom the foot belonged through DNA testing, as well as spatial and temporal profiles based on where and when the shoe arrived, how old the foot is, and when the running shoe was made, he said.

"When dealing with feet, we don't have the luxury of building up a very comprehensive profile, with blue eyes and blond hair. A 16-year-old could have the same size shoe as a 65-year-old," he said.

Fonseca and other coroners will be going over the foot today to ensure that it is human remains, and will then begin compiling information on what they called its "donor." The process could take weeks or months, at which time the data will be compared to missing persons lists, he said.

This foot was found in an inlet near False Creek, a protected body of water, he said, while other feet were found on beaches and nearby islands. He hopes the location of this foot will be helpful to determining its origin.

The investigators are still working to identify the donors of other feet, including a female who had two feet wash up on shore, and a male who had one foot wash up on shore.

"What, why? Um you spent your time at the sleepover searching for gruesome stories on the Internet? I'm going to have to talk to Alix's mother." I stammered

"No. MOM, don't do that! Remember the shoe that I found when we were at Princess Louisa and that man was murdered?"

"Of course I do. But that shoe didn't have a foot in it, did it?"

"No."

"Then this grisly story has nothing to do with your shoe, and I don't want you to dwell on it. You have homework to do now, and you look tired from your sleepover."

Chapter Eleven

Back to Reality

Monday brought with it the usual routine: work, food shopping, meal preparation, school, homework and after-school activities for Katie to be coordinated and organized, workouts for me to fit in, a book-club meeting for the book that I didn't finish because our club chooses books that are either disturbing or challenging—books I would never pick up on my own but am always pleased to read because they are thought-provoking and inspire interesting discussions. Unfortunately, they are hard to read and so occasionally I don't get them finished, or even started, for that matter. This time, having returned only a few weeks before from vacation, you would think I'd have finished the book, but conversation with the many friends and club members we encountered at various anchorages and club outstations had superseded the desire to read. Regardless, it was a good book-club meeting, and even though I couldn't contribute much to the book discussion, I enjoyed hearing about everyone's summer holidays and fall plans.

Friday morning finally arrived; I had to go into the office early as we have a potential new client in Spain who is interested in purchasing our JAG TAGS for their resort. JAG TAGS is my company; it's small, with only five employees including myself, and we design and manufacture designer luggage tags. I know right now you are wondering "Really: is there a market for that?" The answer is "Yes, a small one," and since we are a small company, all is good. High-end resorts, weddings, and corporate functions are our main market. We specialize in the 1950 vintage look: remember those travel stickers people used to plaster all over their luggage and cars? Well, we have an amazing graphic designer who can create any look desired. We'll even do small runs for traveling families or groups who have a logo or crest. It's great for identifying your luggage.

Parking my car in a spot three blocks from my office, I started walking my normal route and was thinking how different everything looks at 6 am. I usually arrived at the office shortly after 8 am, after dropping Katie off at school. This morning, I enjoyed hearing the morning birds that you never hear because the traffic and the general buzz of conversation drown them out, and admiring how the morning light made things I see every day look different—colors crisper, cleaner, with that light dusting of dew, the sky transitioning from the sunrise oranges and pinks to blue. It's hard to define. Still wondering why the time of day should make things look so different, I turned the corner and was crossing the empty street when I saw movement to my left about three quarters of a block down. Surprised and a bit disappointed, since I had been enjoying having the streets to myself, I turned and looked. Police cars blocked the road and yellow tape zigzagged everywhere. Normally I wouldn't have given this a second look or thought, but as it was the building in front of my office, I detoured and went to see what was going on.

Walking up, I saw a group standing around two police cars parked to block the entrance to the building's visitors parking lot. As I approached a very handsome young police officer turned to me and asked If I worked in the building.

"No, the one over there," I replied gesturing in that direction. "What's going on?" I inquired.

He looked in the direction of the other officers who were busy putting up yellow caution tape and interviewing a muscular, grey-haired man, who looked like a security man. The security man was clearly shaken and kept pointing to a blanket on the ground. Something about his expression made me look more closely. I followed his gaze, and as I did so, the coroner lifted a corner and I saw a bloody, gory body lying in a pool of blood, with the distorted face of someone who had died in great pain. The young officer looked at me questioningly and asked if I was okay.

"I'm not squeamish, though I doubt I'll ever forget that...," I replied, trailing off.

"You probably won't," he agreed, then answered my original question: "That unfortunate security guard interrupted a break-in, then pursued the perpetrators out here, where it appears there was a confrontation and he was stabbed multiple times.... We are searching for the murder weapon now." After a hesitation and a shake of his head, he added, "Puzzling; for an office break-in, this is particularly violent." I agreed and was walking away when I heard my named being called. Surprised, because I was sure I hadn't given it out to the officer or anyone, I turned around, and to my astonishment it was Catherine calling me.

"Catherine," I stammered, "what are you doing here?"

"Janeva, thank God you are here!" she replied and ran over to hug me. Astounded, I did the only thing I could and hugged her back. "Thank you for being here," Catherine was sobbing, "you're always here when I need you, thank you." She took my arm and started to lead me back toward the building and past the young police officer, who was now looking at me intently. I can only wonder what he must have been thinking. "Catherine, what's happened?" I demanded.

"I don't know, they called to say that someone had broken into the office... Lorenzo's company,... I mean my company now, apparently. And, and—"

she caught her breath and stumbled as we passed the covered body on the ground, "and the guard is dead, stabbed like Lorenzo. I don't know what to do," she said, pointing and started to collapse.

"Let me help you inside," said the same young officer, taking Catherine's other arm.

Once inside, we all sat down on the comfortable sofa in the reception area. "I'm detective Luke Smythe. Why don't you two tell me how you know each other?" the young officer said. Catherine and I looked at each other in alarm. Where to start? Did he know about her husband's murder on their yacht in a remote cove on the West Coast of Canada? At dinner the night Lorenzo was murdered was the first time we had met, and now I was here at another murder with Catherine! I'm not sure what Catherine was thinking, but that's what went through my head. As the seconds ticked, by I realized one of us had to say something.

"We are both members of the same yacht club," I finally said.

"Okay, that's a start," he said, looking at me with an intensity that made me wonder if he could read minds. At that moment a tall, thin man with thinning salt-and-pepper hair burst into the reception area.

"Catherine, I got your message! What's going on?" he inquired breathlessly. Introductions were made all around; it turned out the man was Frank Duffy, the company COO, and acting CEO since Lorenzo's murder.

"What were they after?" Catherine inquired, much to my amazement, as it was the first logical thing I had ever heard her say.

Frank, dressed in his work outfit of dark dress pants and a white shirt, rubbed his hand over his balding head.

"I have no idea. We don't keep any money in the office," he murmured, shaking his head in bewilderment. He gently put his hand on Catherine's back and said, "Well, we had better go and find out what this is all about." Together they left to assess the damage.

"What is your full name, and can I see some ID?" Detective Smythe demanded of me after they had left. I handed over my driver's license.

"Well, Janeva, I saw that look between you and Catherine. What's this all about?"

I realized that if he didn't know about Lorenzo's murder, a quick Internet search and he soon would, so I told him the whole story. I had just finished when Catherine and Frank returned.

"What did they take?" I inquired.

"Nothing that we could see... they were looking for something in the files and trying to log on to our computer server," Frank said, puzzled. "They all but destroyed our locked filing cabinets, broke into Lorenzo's office, and were going through his computer when the security guard came upon them."

"Oh, NO! I've got to go, my meeting is in 5 min," I
suddenly blurted out, interrupting Frank interesting
narrative. Grabbing my bag off the ground I jumped
up, glanced at Detective Smythe, who nodded okay.
After all, he had my business card, home address,
and cell number if he needed to get hold of me.
Why he would I didn't know; really I had nothing to
do with all this. As these thoughts were going
through my mind, I heard my name called again and
turned to see Catherine running down the street
behind me.

Stopping, I called to her, "Catherine, what are you
doing?"

"Oh Janeva, can I come with you? I really don't
want to stay at Lorenzo's office, and that nice
detective said it was okay."

"Fine, but hurry up, I am already late."

~~~~~~~~~~~~~~~~~~~

An hour later. after my conference call was
finished, I walked out of my office and was
surprised to find Catherine and Frank happily
drinking coffee with Tiffany, my account manager.
Tiffany is highly efficient and very intelligent. This
comes a shock to many people because with her big
blue eyes, flowing mane of blond hair, and petit
figure and she looks like the classic blond bimbo
movie star. It doesn't help that she is from a very
wealthy family and is always dressed in designer
clothes, has weekly manicures and pedicures, not to
mention personal trainers—apparently that's how
she bonds with her mother. After college she was

having trouble getting a job even though she
graduated near the top of her class. Her parents,
fellow Yacht Club members and friends,
approached me and asked if I would be willing to
give her a try. She loves to travel and speaks several
languages. So I did. That was two years ago and
I've never regretted it. Actually I'm amazed that
she's still with me: with her ability and potential she
should be working for a multinational. But I do
have a trump card: her fiancé, Cory, is my graphic
designer/ computer expert. I know most companies
don't approve of internal relationships but I see
JAG TAGS as a family business, and both Cory and
Tiffany as family. So far it has all worked out well,
and if things change at some future date, well, we'll
deal with it then.

"Welcome back, Tiffany, how was Provence?"

"Really good; I think I have some solid leads. How
did the Spain call go?" Tiffany asked me in her
singsong voice.

"Great! Good job finding them, Tiff, we're moving
forward with art proofs. It sounds like there's lots of
future potential for us because they have sister
properties throughout Europe and in the Caribbean.
I told them you would be following up."

Standing up, Tiffany said, "I'll just go over to
Cory's office, to go over the artwork with him,"
giving me a coy smile.

Turning to Catherine and Frank, I said, "Let me get
a coffee, then you can give me an update." What I
really wanted to say was "Why are you two still

here?!"

Returning from our small coffee room (well, it's more of a closet but it does the job), I said "Come into the meeting room" and gestured in that direction, closing the door behind us I sat across from them at the small table we use for meetings.

Sipping my coffee I looked from one to the other. Silence. Catherine looked at me in a pleading sort of way, and Frank was busy examining his pen.

Groaning inwardly, as I hate it when I have to take charge, I asked, "Catherine, have you been here the whole time?" She nodded in the affirmative. "Frank, what happened after we left?"

Heaving a sigh, Frank started reluctantly to speak.

"Janeva, I'm sorry to drag you into this," he began, then added more cheerfully, "but it seems that you are already somewhat involved as a good friend of Catherine's." This was news to me. "And you were there when Lorenzo was murdered," he continued.

"Okay…and what is it you don't want to tell Catherine?" I asked as it hit me: Frank needed me to buffer the bad news and support Catherine.

"We are broke!" he exclaimed, with a thud like a heavy rock falling to the ground.

"Awk!" was all that Catherine managed to say, and then, after a long silence, "But we have money—Lorenzo had family money!"

"I'm sorry, Catherine, but Lorenzo committed all his liquid assets to Dexia; we have this exciting new product and were so close to releasing it."

"Oh my God,... what am I going to do?" cried Catherine.

"I'm sorry, Catherine," Frank repeated sadly.

"What about the yacht?"

"I'm afraid you will have to sell that too, whenever it's released from Canada. Unfortunately we need the money now. We are in dire straits...I've been stalling paying bills, waiting, but now..." Frank trailed off.

"I sold the boat: it's coming down from Canada on Sunday, and the new owner is going to take possession on Monday, after the cleaning and mechanical crew go all through it," Catherine added hopefully. "The money will be in our account by end of day Monday...will that help??"

"Oh, thank heavens! What wonderful news! We will need that money to cover payroll and office lease, loan payment and your house."

"My house?!" Catherine squeaked, looking panicked.

He groaned, "Catherine?... You knew, didn't you, that Lorenzo put your house up as collateral for our line of credit? But with the money from the yacht sale we'll be able to pay off the line of credit and you will have clear title to you house again." Frank looked at Catherine, clearly astonished that she didn't know about the house.

Could Catherine be the killer? The startling but illuminating thought flashed into my mind. She hated boating, and now it turned out that selling the boat solved all her financial problems. I wanted to follow this intriguing logic further, but I suddenly realized that both Catherine and Frank were staring at me, so I quickly asked, "When I met Lorenzo, he didn't act or look like someone who was facing financial ruin. Plus he told us in great detail about future yacht trips he had planned on the Atlantis— he seemed to loved that boat!" I looked at Frank and Catherine in turn, then continued, "The financial position of the company can't have been a surprise?!"

"No, of course not! We were at the very last stage of a financing round, and if Lorenzo hadn't died the money would be in the bank by now and all would be well, but the investors are understandably spooked by Lorenzo's death and everything's been put on hold," Frank explained.

"Oh." My mind was processing the implications. "So your options are go bankrupt or use the money from the boat?"

"That is correct. Well, there is one other option, though it's an unpleasant one to me, but with Lorenzo's death it's one we have to consider. One of our investors, John Blackwood, has suggested that we sell the company. To that end he has even implied that he has a buyer," added Frank.

"Interesting," I said.

"I know; it's just that the new product is set to be released next week," said Frank with emotion.

"I'm sorry, Frank, but I don't get it," said Catherine

quietly.

"Yes I think we need more detail," I added.

"We have this great new product that's just about to launch.... Anyway, if we sell the company now, we'll have to sell if for our current valuation. But if we can hang on for just one more week, until 'E-lett'—that's what we're calling the new product—is launched, then the company will be worth three times as much as it is today." Frank took a sip of his coffee, then made a face as it had turned cold. Continuing, he said, "It's revolutionary, and all our customers have said they will buy it because it's an obvious add-on to our current product line." He reached down and pulled a stack of papers out of his brief case to show me.

"What's so special about your new product?" I asked Catherine. She looked uncomfortable, then shook her head and looked out of the window.

Frank jumped in with "We have developed a new computer chip... for the next version of our already very successful loyalty card app for Mac and Android phones. The thing is that this new computer chip is really cool. We think it will revolutionize the industry; it could change computing as we know it."

"Loyalty card app?" I asked, grasping at the one thing I understood. Computer chips are beyond me, but loyalty card I know.

"I see you have your purse with you?" he said, gesturing at that item. "Please, can you take out your wallet?"

I did as was requested.

"Now, most women have a stack of loyalty cards—
for coffee, hair products, Costco, pet store,
stationary store, food store—"

"Okay, you can stop now," I said, holding up a
stack of the cards he had just mentioned.

"Most men have some of the same cards, though
their cards tend to be for electronics, sports, airline
mileage, cars, rental car memberships, and hotel
club memberships."

Nodding in agreement, I thought of Thomas's slim
wallet, and of how many times he had called or
texted me from a hotel reception desk asking for his
Hilton or Fairmont Presidents club number over the
years.

Holding up his iPhone, Frank opened an app and
proceeded to show me how he had all his cards
stored electronically. "You see how both the front
and back of the card show up on the screen? The
front is important because it has the logo and in
some cases your photo, but the back is the key.
Notice the bar code?"

We nodded. Clearly this was new to Catherine also.
Looking at her in surprise, I wondered how could
she have not known what her husband did for a
living. My next thought was to wonder how many
wives had no real concept of what their husbands
did at work all day. I was about to explore that
avenue of thought further when Frank handed me

back my phone, on which he had downloaded the Dexia app.

"Take one of your cards with a bar code on the back. Now open the Dexia app and follow the onscreen instructions," Frank said.

I picked my Costco card first.

Shaking his head but smiling, he said, "Not that one—notice that it has a electronic strip on the back, not a bar code?"

Surprised, as I hadn't noticed that before, I picked my CVS pharmacy card instead and followed the simple instructions. Using my iPhone camera, I lined up the card to fit in the square the app highlighted on my phone, and took a photo of the front and back of the card

"That's it?" I asked, looking at the small image shown on my phone of the front and back of my CVS card.

"Well, yes and no" Frank said with a smile. "Yes, you can now use that at CVS instead of your card; they can scan the bar code from your phone."

"This is great" I exclaimed. "I hate carrying all these cards."

"The next step is for you to go onto our website. You can do it through the app on your phone and set up your secure account."

"Why?"

"What if your phone or wallet was lost or stolen?

All your cards are stored in our cloud now. The advantages of this are that you can easily access and manage all your loyalty cards in one location. When you move, or change your phone number, it's no problem. Just log on to your Dexia account and do the update; or, if you want to see how far you are from a bonus—whether it's a free hotel night or a free cup of coffee—now you can access all that info through your Dexia account."

"Sweet," I said, as I took a photo of my Safeway card. "But what about the new product you mentioned?"

I will need you to sign this nondisclosure from first; sorry, but the launch is next week, and you know…"

"Of course," I said. as I quickly scanned the legal document, then signed it.

"Our new product is called 'E-lett,' as I mentioned, and it's the next evolution of the Dexia app you were just using. The Costco card you pulled out we couldn't scan because of the magnetic code on the back. Correct?"

I agreed, looking at my Costco card and wishing it could be scanned, as several times I have arrived at Costco only to realize the card was in my other purse and not with me. How frustrating!

"We've figured out how to easily transfer the data on the magnetic strip located on the back of your credit cards and convert it to a format that store scanners can read. We have been working closely with the major credit card companies to ensure the security."

"But why would the credit card companies be interested?" I interrupted.

"Excellent question: I'm glad you asked. The credit card companies are worried that online payment methods like PayPal and Google Wallet will start to erode their business as more and more people use their phones for transactions. Second, our system is very secure. Transactions are protected by thumbprints and passwords,, so even if your phone gets stolen or lost the thief would have to know your password and have your thumb. This one feature alone will save the credit card industry millions in fraudulent transactions. Third, if your phone gets misplaced you can log on to your secure cloud wallet through our Dexia website and put all your cards on hold until you phone turns up; or if it truly is stolen, you can order new cards from the site, saving you time and many phone calls. Of course, like our original product, you can easily make address changes, click through to vendor sites to make payments, or check account status."

"Wow, that is really great and exciting! I will definitely use your product," I said.

"What this company is offering to acquire us now would just cover our debts, credit lines, and what we owe our investors to date. So, you see, we need enough operating cash for the next few months. What's really exciting is the computer chip we developed as we explored better and more secure ways of processing and securing the credit card data. We need time to explore this and flush out its potential. Lorenzo felt that this chip was a game changer, and I agree with him. If Lorenzo was correct about this chip, Catherine will be able to sell this company for enough profit to keep her in the style she has become accustomed to."

Catherine brightened at this. Suddenly I realized I was falling way behind on my day's work. Not knowing what else to do, I remarked, "Well, Frank, you've given Catherine a lot to think about, and I really need to get back to work." I ended the impromptu meeting, told Catherine I would see her at the club, and went to relieve my frazzled-looking receptionist, who was holding a stack of documents for me to review and indicating that there were many messages in my voice mail.

Chapter Twelve

Finally the Weekend

I finally got out of the office, and went home to pack for Katie and me. Thomas had already packed, so all I had to do was grab his bag. Next I went to the store to grab some food for the boat. As we were just going to Geranium Island on Saturday for the one night, I didn't need much, dinner tonight would be at the Yacht Club, so all I needed was food for two breakfasts and lunches and the group barbeque Saturday night on the dock.

Next I picked Katie up from her friend's house, then Thomas up from his office. The club has limited parking, so we make a real effort to use only one car, plus they give us a hard time when you ask for two weekend parking passes. This had the added benefit of Thomas helping load up the wheelbarrow and wheeling it with our groceries and suitcases down to the boat. Well, it worked up to a point. He was great until I got everything down below. Then he announced that as he didn't really know where anything went and the galley was so small, he would just wander up to the clubhouse to see if Greg or Kevin were there.

"Can I go too, Mom? I've unpacked my bag and I want a rematch at foosball with Sam," Katie pleaded.

Sam was Kevin's handsome fifteen-year-old son. All the young girls at the club were in love with him, and Katie, who had known Sam her whole life, loved to show off what good friends they were.

"Oh, okay," I said to them both, and, to Thomas, "Order me a margarita; I'll need one after I've done all this by myself."

"Done. See you in a bit" from Thomas, and "Thanks, Mom" from Katie, they answered cheerfully, ignoring the sarcasm as they hurried away before I could find more any work for them to do.

Actually, I didn't mind. I enjoyed the quiet with them gone. I could take my time and put everything away just as I like it. I'm one of those people who prefers everything to be neat and tidy. I sleep so much better when the house or boat is clean. Okay! Maybe it's a bit over the top, but cleaning really is so satisfying. I love to look around the house or boat and see everything uncluttered and in its exact right spot. Eventually, I was done, the food was put away, and our clothing was hung up in our locker. My shoes were stowed away, nice and neat, in pairs, just as I like them. I looked in Katie's cabin... then closed the door; what a disaster. Tomorrow, once we arrived at Geranium Island, she would have to tidy up before she went off to hang out with her friends.

I was pleased to see Thomas had snagged the best table on the deck outside the Yacht Club's restaurant/lounge. Already there were Greg, Step, Kevin and his new date Felicia. As usual, she was a gorgeous brunette and 15 years too young for Kevin. As much as I enjoy how much a new person can add to the conversation, it was always a struggle, because you never knew how long Kevin would keep them around. Kevin's personality was very attractive to women. He had them fighting over him...perhaps the luxury downtown loft and 50-foot yacht helped. Also at the table, to my surprise, were Tiffany and Cody. As soon as I sat down I found out why Tiffany and Cody were with us, instead of their regular group of twenty-somethings, who hung out in the games room and had claimed the far corner table as their own.

"Janeva, I'm just dying to know what this morning was all about," said Tiffany in her sweet singsong voice. She had changed from her work clothes into yachting haute couture, and looked like an add for Nautica. With his short-cropped brown hair and football physique, Cody matched her perfectly. He smiled at her and looked over at me. So did the rest of the group. Clearly they had been speculating in my absence.

Steph pored me a margarita from the pitcher. "Really, Janeva. How does your path keep crossing with Catherine's in such a dramatic way?"

"I know," I said, looking around. "I keep expecting her to pop up." Everyone laughed. I continued, "As long as you all promise to keep this to yourselves. I know it will all come out anyway, but I'd rather it didn't come from me." I then gave a detailed description of my morning. Everyone was incredulous about the stabbing.

"What's the world coming to—stabbings, murders—I'm moving!" pronounced Kevin. We all laughed at him, because it was a typical Kevin response.

"Let's order dinner then I'll tell you the rest," I continued.

"There's more?!" exclaimed Steph.

"Yes, but you'll have to wait until I check on Katie. She must be having a good time or she would have joined us by now. But if she doesn't eat she will raid the fridge when we get back to the boat and we won't have any snacks for the weekend." Looking at Thomas, I asked him to order me the crispy Thai chicken salad and went downstairs to the games room, where Katie was having a great time playing ping pong with a group of other Yacht Club kids.

I ordered a burger and fries for her...I would have preferred something healthier, but it was what all the other kids were eating, so I vowed (to myself) to feed her lots of salad and veggies for the rest of the weekend. I was just coming around the corner from the stairway when I heard Catherine's now familiar voice.

I stopped and waited to see if Catherine was heading upstairs. She was.... Perhaps if I walked slowly enough, she wouldn't see me. I followed her at a distance and was relieved to see that she didn't head out to the deck but to a far corner of the lounge. Arriving at our table, I wasn't surprised to see that Tiffany and Cody had left, but I was disappointed to see that Trent and Wiffy Braise-Bottom the Third had taken their spots. I realized that I would have to wait to tell the group the rest of the story about Lorenzo's company's financial problems, sale of the Atlantis, and its return from Canada this weekend. The group was in mid-discussion about one of the Yacht Club outstations. Apparently it needed new docks, and this was causing a great deal of debate about what type they should be—wood or concrete. Finally the food arrived, and more margaritas, and after a pleasant evening we headed back to the boat.

"Someone has been going through our stuff!" I said, as I opened my hanging locker to take out my pajamas. We had closed up the boat when we went up to the clubhouse for dinner but hadn't locked it, as was our custom. The Yacht Club marina is secure and only members can access it.

 "What are you talking about?" Thomas replied grumpily.

"Look: my shoes have been moved and the stuff in my bag has been moved," I said, looking around.

"How about your stuff?" I asked him.

"Looks fine to me. You're imagining things,...I'm tired," was his response as he climbed into bed.

It looked to me like his clothes had been rifled and his shoes moved around, but this was because they looked neater than usual. Normally Thomas just tossed his shoes into the closet, but now they looked like they were in pairs. But this was inconclusive, so I did a check of the boat. Katie was in her head (or bathroom), and our head looked as usual.

The galley was tidy and everything was stowed away, ready for breakfast in the morning. The salon or living room looked the same at first glance, but as I studied it, waiting for Katie, I realized that the throw pillows weren't in the right positions. Why would someone move the pillow around unless they wanted to get into the storage hatches underneath the settee?

I turned to check the large hanging locker in the main salon, where we keep our wet weather gear, tables and chairs for the dock, and other miscellaneous things, and it had definitely been searched, though I couldn't find anything missing. The TV, computers, and electronics were all still there. I checked, and none of the alcohol was missing.

Katie's cabin was in its usual cluttered state, the bed full of stuffed animals, her shelf with books and board games, and her dresser top full of felts, pencil crayons, glitter glue, glitter tattoos, beads, string for friendship bracelets, sea shells, beach glass, craft paper, and scissors, all in various containers. The dresser has a lip around it, but it is still a complete mystery to me why everything doesn't go flying around as the boat moves through waves or we heel from one side to the next. My only surmise is that the space is so full and crowded that there is no place for anything to move. In any case, it was imposable to tell whether Katie's cabin had been searched. So I said good night to her and went to bed.

Chapter Thirteen

Geranium Island

After a quick breakfast of toast and coffee the next morning, we set sail. Our friends Greg and Steph and Kevin and his son, Sam, in their power boats were still sound asleep when we left because it takes us much longer to get anywhere. We sail at an average of 6 knots, less if there is light wind, whereas the power boats go 18 to 20 knots, so it takes us three times longer, and that's only if the wind is blowing the right direction. If, like today, it's not, well, at least it's a beautiful sunny day and it is windy, so we will enjoy the sail and get to the island in time for cocktails.

Katie and I tried to read our books, but Thomas was determined to race various other sailboats who had no idea they were racing us, so every time we got comfortable he either tacked or wanted the sails adjusted. Katie and I finally gave up on reading when he announced that he wanted us to hoist the

Gennaker, a sail like a spinnaker but easier to sail with only three people, one being Katie, who is a reluctant sailor at best. It requires constant adjustments but is really fun to fly. Arriving at last, we were pleased to see that Kevin had positioned his boat on the dock in a way to ensure that we had a spot with the group.

Nonboaters do the same thing with their cars, like when someone parks their car mostly in one spot but partly in the next spot as well, thus making it impossible for anyone to park that spot. Kevin, his son Sam, and Greg each grabbed a line and walked Kevin's boat back 5 feet, tied it off, then caught our lines. We were to have a late lunch, as we had missed a dock lunch with the group earlier. I moved our deck chairs to the dock, opened a bottle of white wine, handed Thomas a beer and some turkey dogs to BBQ, brought out some cut veggies and hummus, and voila, lunch on the dock. After lunch Katie and Sam went up the dock to the field to play some Frisbee. I cleaned up the lunch dishes, then went to join Steph and Kevin on the dock. "Where is Thomas?" I asked, sitting down.

"Where do you think?" Steph said, waving at their boat, where the engine cover was raised.

"Oh" I said knowingly. "a project is afoot." Turning to Kevin I asked, "How do you resist?"

"What? And ruin my clothes mucking around with an engine? No, I'm no fool; I'd much rather sit here visiting with you two lovely ladies," he said with a smile, then gallantly filled our glasses with the crisp white Sauvignon Blanc.

"So tell us about your new date,... she didn't come?" I inquired, and we proceeded to analyze Kevin's latest relationships until Greg and Thomas reappeared, very pleased with themselves for having resolved the engine problem, something about the impeller.

"For you, Janeva," Greg said, handing me a set of elbow-length 1950s-style rubber gloves.

"But where is the bleach?" I replied, laughing and putting on the gloves. "Clearly my love of spray Clorox bleach has not gone unnoticed."

"Some women use air freshener with nice pine or lemon smells, but not my Janeva: she goes for the ultra-clean bleach smell," said Thomas.

"Well, I would rather have that than the cigarette smell our boat had last night when we returned. I can't for the life of me figure out where the smell came from.... It was almost like someone had been on our boat," said Greg, puzzled.

I sat up, immediately alert. "Really? I was convinced that someone had searched our boat, but nothing was missing."

"Why did you think your boat had been searched, and do you know what they were looking for?" Greg asked.

"No idea what they were looking for, but I think it had to do with clothes or shoes."

Groaning, Thomas interjected "Really, WHO would want to steal your shoes?"

Ignoring this obvious jibe, I continued to answer Greg's question: "My hanging locker door was ajar, the settee throw cushions were not the right—it was like when you and Thomas go digging for tools and stuff in the storage bins."

"And all that time I was sooo careful to put the throw pillows back just so!" interjected Thomas, again with sarcasm.

"Thomas, you're not taking this seriously!" I scolded.

"Well, what does throw-pillow positioning have to do with shoes, and do you think there is a deranged cigarette-smoking Yacht Club member with a shoe fetish? This is a ridiculous conversation," he continued.

Rolling my eyes at him, I continued, "No. But someone did break into Lorenzo's office yesterday morning, then last night when we were at dinner someone went through my hanging locker—well, shoes, anyway. I couldn't tell if he went through yours or Katie's as they are too messy to start with."

Thomas interrupted me. "Two totally different events. Lorenzo's office break-in was in all probability some druggie looking for the petty cash or, if you really want to go out on a limb, perhaps someone interested in their intellectual property. But I'm just asking—how could that possibly have anything to do with shoe rifling?"

I suddenly realized that I hadn't told them about the financial crisis that Lorenzo's company was facing;

I was about to repeat the conversation I had had with Catherine and Frank the day before in my office, when Steph said something that completely distracted me. What she said was:

"Could whoever went through your closet and left the lingering cigar smell on our boat have been looking for that shoe Katie found, floating in the water beside the dock, the day Lorenzo was murdered?"

This statement dropped like a stone in a calm pool of water, sending ripples of surprise out from it. We all looked at each other in silence. "I had completely forgotten about that," was all I could manage to say.

"Katie will know where the shoe is," said Thomas logically. "But I really can't imagine what significance a shoe can have," he added.

"Where is Katie?" I asked looking around. "Last time I saw her she was doing cartwheels, handsprings, and back walkovers in the field" I added, looking in that direction

"Well, let's go find her," said Kevin jumping up and marching down the dock, leaving the rest of us to chase after him. At the top of the ramp Kevin, again in his take-charge manner, said, "Let's spread out, she can't be far."

"I'll take the back field," said Steph, heading off that way.

The rest of us followed suit, going in different directions. "Rendezvous back here in 20 min," yelled Kevin, as he headed toward the coffee shop, Thomas to walk the docks, and I went to walk up the street of the small village of Cedar Grove. Clearly whoever did the naming of this area just looked around and picked the first two things he saw: geraniums as in naming of Geranium Island, and cedar trees for the village of Cedar Grove. I had to laugh to myself. As I quickly walked passed one of my favorite stores, "Island Treasures," I couldn't help glancing in the window because they always had such cute stuff. The residents of Geranium Island are very crafty, or maybe I should say artsy—okay, let's settle for talented. From hand-crafted driftwood salad bowls and dishes to pottery, art, clothing, etc., I almost always fell in love with some knick-knack whenever I went into that store. But not today. Right now we had to find Katie and get to the bottom of the Shoe Mystery. There had to be something about that shoe. Otherwise, why had our boats been searched?

Well, Katie was not in the corner grocery, nor had she been, according to the checkout clerk. Looking at my watch I realized that 17 minutes had passed and I had better head back to Kevin's rendezvous. Past experience had taught me that the abuse I would face if I was late wasn't worth it, and I was sure one of the group would have found Katie.

"What, no Katie?!" I asked in surprise, looking around at the concerned faces of the group.

"We hoped you had found her!" said Thomas with distress.

"Where could she be? How could she disappear on this small island?" I exclaimed. I was trying to stay calm, but that feeling of fear and dread, that something might really have happened to her, was starting to overwhelm me.

Thomas, who knows me better than anyone else, said to me in his stern CEO tone, "Don't panic, stay calm: we need to think right now."

It worked, even though that tone irritated me, since I'm not one of his employees and this wasn't a work crisis, it was about his daughter.

"Ok, what do you propose we do?" I snarled, looking around frantically. "We just searched for her!"

"True, and now we are going to search again. She is a smart girl and I can't believe she would just wander off with someone with out telling us. Plus, look around. This place is packed with tourists. She would have screamed if she had been grabbed or forcibly taken," Thomas said logically.

"Oh my God,... the ferry!" Kevin whispered.

We all turned as one to look at the slow-moving line of cars off to the left of where we were standing, at the end of the main street of Cedar Grove. Cedar Grove is one of those picturesque villages that consists of one main street that starts at the ferry dock, lined with shops mostly of the tourist variety but including a coffee shop, pub, and diner, and ending at the corner grocery. The marina is mid-town, in a small bay, with the ferry dock on the left and a park on the right with a gazebo in the field where community events and picnics are held. The main dock ramp comes up to this field, then there is a picturesque path that wraps around to the ferry dock where the cars were loading on the ferry!

"We have to stop the ferry!" I cried and started to run toward the dock.

"Wait!! You'll never get there in time!" Kevin yelled after me. Stopping and almost in tears, I had to admit he was right. "We need to call the police and have the ferry searched at the other side. Thomas where is your phone?!" I demanded.

"Hold on and calm down, Janeva," said Greg in his professional doctor voice. "We don't even know that Katie is on that ferry. She could have found a friend and gone to their boat, or be in a store. Did you check them all?"

"Of course not, there wasn't time," I snapped.

Thomas put his hand on my shoulder and pulled me into a hug. "Janeva. Take a deep breath. We will search again, this time look everywhere. We have 40 minutes until the ferry reaches the dock on the other side, so let's split up and meet back here in 30 minutes. That way we will still have time to call the police if we haven't found her."

A half hour later, we met up at the rendezvous, a sad and shocked group.

Thomas had his phone out and was about to dial when—

"Janeva, Thomas—it's Katie!.... There she is!"

yelled Steph, pointing up the street.

We all turned and, yes, there she was walking down the street, smiling and chatting to Tiffany.

I ran up to her and hugged and hugged her again. "Where have you been, we have been searching the whole island for you!" I demanded.

"Mom, what's wrong? I was only with Tiff, " replied Katie, looking bewildered.

"I'm so sorry, Janeva," said Tiffany, looking very confused. "We saw Katie on the lawn and she walked up to the store with us."

Cody had just walked up behind them, his arms full of bags.

"Katie, of course it's okay for you to be with Tiffany and Cody, but it's not okay for you to go off without letting your mother and me know where you are going!" scolded Thomas.

At the emotion in his words and the reprimand, Katie immediately broke into tears. I hugged her even tighter. "Your father is right. You had us running all over the island; we were just about to call the police."

"The police!" Tiffany and Katie said in unison.

"Yes, young lady," Kevin jumped in. "We thought you had been abducted and were on the ferry in some car!"

"Abducted on Geranium Island?" said Cody in surprise.

"I know we overreacted, but after Lorenzo's

murder, the break-in at his office, and our boats being searched last night…," I replied, still hugging Katie.

"Mom, you're squishing me, she whined, and wriggled free, only to be hugged by her dad.

"When did you guys get here?" Greg asked Tiffany and Cody. Looking at her watch, Tiffany answered, "I don't know; about 45 minutes ago."

"And you've already managed to buy that much stuff?" said Steph, shaking her head.

"Tiff can out-shop anyone!" Cody replied.

"Cody—that's not true," Tiffany pouted. "We were here a few weeks ago and I ordered the cutest stuff for our guest bathroom. The store just called this morning to say it was ready."

Looking at the bags, Steph said, "'Island Treasures'—I love the stuff from that store. What did you get?"

Rolling his eyes as Tiffany started to dig through the bags, Kevin ordered us all back to the dock if we were going to unpack bags.

Later, I followed Katie topside (on deck) after our family meeting and a reestablishment of the rules. I had to laugh as I looked at all Tiffany's purchases, spread out before her.

Steph was oohing and ahhing over a handmade soap-dish in the shape of a rowboat painted blue, with oars, and a matching toothbrush holder made to look like a lighthouse, matching blue and white

towels, bath mats, and then there were the clothes.
Oh how I wish I had Tiffany's shopping budget. On
second thought, even if I did, really, where would I
put everything?

"Okay, enough about clothes.... What about the
shoe that started this all?" boomed Kevin.

Turning to Katie I asked, "Honey, do you remember
that shoe you found in Princes Louisa?"

"Of course I do, Mom," she retorted, like I had
asked her something that was clearly obvious.

"Great," I replied, refusing to be dragged into an
argument. She was clearly still upset about our
earlier reaction to her wandering off with Tiffany.
"Where is it?"

"In my room," she replied blandly.

"At home or on the boat?" I persevered.

"Here."

"Really?" I replied, surprised because I hadn't seen
it when I looked in her room. But I was clever
enough not to say that. Instead I asked, "Could you
run and get it? We would like to have a look at it."

She shrugged and went off to get the shoe.

When she returned, it was clear to me why I hadn't
seen the shoe. The white shoe was covered—and I
mean every inch of it was covered—with glitter
glue and colored felt pen doodles, and the opening
of the shoe, where your foot would normally go in,
was full of felt pens and other colored ballpoint
pens. Put on her desktop with all her other crafts,

miscellaneous toys, and stuffed animals, I could see how both our intruder and I had missed it. When she handed it to me I took out the pens, giving them back to her and asking her to put them in her room. I turned the shoe around and looked inside and under it, but it just looked like a ordinary, if highly decorated, shoe to me. At this point I had to hand it over to Thomas, who was hovering above me, wanting his turn to discover what mysteries the shoe might hold.

The shoe was dutifully passed around to Kevin then Greg, Steph, Cody, Tiffany, Sam, and to Katie, who had been filled in by now as to why we were SO interested in her shoe, then finally back to me. Anyone watching would have smiled or laughed to themselves as they saw seven adults and two teenagers, sitting on folding chairs on the dock or boatside, and even on the raised edge of the dock, playing a strange "pass the glittering shoe" game, each person more eager than the last to get his or her hands on the shoe. As we got more desperate we started to dismantle the shoe, which was no small task. After the sole was lifted out and showed no secret compartment, like some Nike shoes have for pedometer inserts, we realized that a more determined approach was required.

As Kevin, Sam, Greg, Cody Katie, and Tiffany went off in search of tools that might help us dismantle the shoe, Steph and I went off to our own boats—to make bruschetta and tortilla chips with dip in Steph's case, and strawberry-banana blender drinks in mine. I made the first batch as virgin nonalcoholic drinks for Katie and Sam, who had been coaxed away from his video games for now to join us.

Chapter Fourteen

Dismantling a Shoe

The shoe dismantlement was temporarily halted as appetizers and drinks were consumed, while the discussion was all about what a shoe could possibly hide.

"It must be drugs," suggested Kevin.

"Really. And how much could you store in a shoe, Dad?" retorted Sam.

"I don't know—coke or crack? You don't need much of that to make the shoe valuable."

"A secret message," suggested Katie.

"Perhaps it's a prototype shoe," suggested Steph.

"Looks ordinary to me," responded her husband Greg, as he turned the shoe around and held it up to the light. As he stared at the bottom he said, "What about electronics?"

"Yes, a flash drive!" agreed Thomas. "We need to be very careful dismantling this shoe."

And so the discussion went, until the food was cleared away, drinks refilled, and we were able to convince Tiffany and Cody to join us for dinner. I love to cook and always make way too much food, so I usually had to find a creative way to reuse any leftovers in a new recipe as my family doesn't eat leftovers. I know, "Eye Roll," but it's really my own fault as I keep cooking up new things. Actually, I enjoy the challenge of turning leftover ribs into pulled pork for burritos, or leftover chicken into chicken pot pie, etc.

I took out the pre-marinated steaks to get them to room temperature and made a béchamel sauce (Katie's favorite) with garlic and tarragon from my herb garden for the homemade pasta (Thomas's favorite) that I had made at home and bought with us. I boiled the pasta water, turning it down to a simmer until just before we were ready to eat, since homemade pasta only takes 3 to 4 minutes to cook. I went up top to see how Steph's salad and garlic bread were coming along. Kevin, as usual, was providing the wine. He has an amazing wine cellar.

I burst out laughing as I took in the scene below me on the dock. Thomas had the shoe in clamps that he and Cody were holding secure as Greg the doctor was carefully using his scalpel to cut the shoe apart. Kevin was kneeling in with pliers and a wrench, holding apart the areas that Greg was carefully cutting, and Sam was holding a powerful flashlight above them. Katie was sitting behind Greg and handing him various surgical instruments and tools, as he required them. Turning, I went to go and find my camera. This was a photo opportunity not to be missed.

After taking a few photos with no one even looking up at me, I said, "Okay, everyone look up at me!" This was greeted with "Shhhh!" and "We're busy!" Giving up, I looked across to see Steph and Tiffany appear with a huge salad and garlic bread. They also laughed, and were in turn told to "Be quiet," so we three looked on in amazed delight.

Realizing that this was going to take a while, I returned to turn off my pasta water and uncorked one of the bottles of Pinot Noir that Kevin had kindly deposited in our cockpit. I poured three glasses, waved to Steph and Tiffany to come join me, and we settled down to sip the lovely wine as we watched and photographed the careful dismantlement of a shoe.

"I found it!" exclaimed Greg, holding up a impossibly thin, one-inch by half-inch semi-clear piece of plastic between his index finger and thumb.

"Great, but what is it?" several of us asked in unison.

"Maybe it's a pedometer," Sam said, holding out his hand. "No,… I guess not," he admitted as he scrutinized the object.

"I agree it's not a pedometer; look at the pattern…

actually I'm 99 percent sure it's a computer chip of sorts," Thomas said, taking the small plastic object and holding it up to the light to examine it closely.

"Really? It doesn't look like one. It just looks like a some extra plastic was accidently added in the sole of this shoe," Cody said.

"You have to look closely to see the transistors— see?" Thomas shone the flashlight at the small piece of plastic and we all crowded in to look.

"Ouch!" came a chorus as several of us hit heads trying to see.

"Let's take turns," I said, standing and rubbing my head. My turn finally came; it seemed to take forever as we had to look one at a time, with Thomas holding the small piece of semi-clear plastic that everyone now agreed was some kind of computer chip.

"But why would someone imbed a computer chip, flash drive, or any other type of electronic in a running shoe?" Steph asked, with a shake of her head.

"That is an excellent question, and this isn't just any computer chip," said Thomas, our computer expert. "It's unlike anything I've ever seen before."

"What do you mean?" Greg asked.

"Well, for starters it's not made of silicon; this material is so thin, and even more interesting, it's flexible."

"I don't get it," said Katie.

"A silicon chip is a piece of almost pure silicon, usually less than one centimeter square and about half a millimeter thick. A silicon computer chip contains millions of transistors—a transistor being a device that controls the flow of electric current—and other tiny electronic circuit components, packed and interconnected in layers beneath the surface. There is a grid of thin metallic wires on the surface of the chip, which is used to make electrical connections to other devices. This tiny component is responsible for arithmetic, logic, and/or memory functions in a computer.

"The silicon chip was developed independently by two engineers: Jack Kilby of Texas Instruments in 1958, and Robert Noyce of Fairchild Semiconductor in 1959. In addition to being used in computers, smart phones and tablets, silicon chips are used in calculators, microwave ovens, automobile radios and engine controllers, DVD players, TV, video games, and toys. We use them every day," explained Thomas in a preoccupied manner, as he continued to study the piece of plastic, "but this isn't silicon."

"Then what is it?" several of us asked at once, though not at quite the same time, so that it came out as a jumble.

"Hmmm. I wonder. Graphene,…could this possible be graphene?" Thomas said slowly as he turned and flexed the object in question.

"What is graphene?" again we all asked, and moved in closer to him to hear, spilling a drink in the process.

Starting out of his almost trance-like state, Thomas said, "If this is graphene and someone has figured out how to cost-effectively use it as a computer chip, instead of using silicon... just think of the possibilities...," and a preoccupied look came over his face as he did just that.

"THOMAS!" I exclaimed. "What is graphene and why is it important?"

"It's flexible, for starters," he replied in an It's obvious voice. Noticing that we were all still staring at him uncomprehendingly, he sighed and continued, "If graphene chips replaced the silicon chip—and by the looks of this, someone has figured out how to do that—it will take wearable computing to a whole new level."

"Cool; I get it!" Sam piped up. "Wristwatch computers—or computerized clothing, or roll-up iPads!" Taking out his iPhone, he quickly googled graphene: "Wikipedia says: 'Graphene is a substance composed of pure carbon, with atoms arranged in a regular hexagonal pattern similar to graphite, but in a one-atom thick sheet.'... WOW; this is technical stuff," he trailed off, scrolling with his finger through screen after screen. "My gosh, you would have to have a Ph.D. in computer science or computer engineering to understand all this!"

At this point Thomas, who does have a Ph.D. in computer science, interjected with "What makes graphene so exciting is that, as you can see, it's not only thin and flexible but it's 40+ times stronger than steel, plus it's a semiconductor whose electrical conductivity is 1000 times better than silicon's. And that's just the start of its fascinating properties. For example, a group in Barcelona thinks it can be used to make ultra-sensitive low-cost photo detectors."

"What is a photo detector?" Katie asked.

"A device that converts light to electricity. It's used in digital cameras, night vision gear, biomechanical images and telecom equipment. This group in Barcelona is spraying nanometers or quantum dots of lead sulfide crystals on the graphene."

"Thomas, stop. You're way over our heads. We really don't care about the wonders of graphene. What I am interested in why it's in that shoe, and is that small chip what Lorenzo was murdered for?" I interrupted him mid-lecture.

"Janeva's right. We could be in real danger if this piece of plastic was what got Lorenzo killed," Steph cried out in alarm.

"You are both correct, of course. I expect it's not just what this chip is made of that's important, but what's on it. We need to get this"—he held up the plastic chip—"to my office so I can start working on it." Then he tucked the chip into his wallet.

"Shouldn't we take it to the police?" Kevin inquired.

"Humph… technically, yes. But it's a Canadian investigation, and how would we get it safely to them, for starters? If we dropped it off at our local police station, I truly doubt they would know what to do with it. I think we should let Thomas's team of computer geniuses find out what's on it; then we will better know what to do," Greg answered.

"Right: Lorenzo was an American, and whatever is on this chip could be... I don't know, a state secret," I agreed.

"I hadn't thought of that. Should it go to the FBI or the CIA or the Canadian Police?" Kevin rejoined.

"Okay, okay; we are all agreed. I'll see if I can decode this chip, then we'll send it to the proper authorities. Now: what happened to dinner? I'm starved. Is anyone else hungry?" Thomas pronounced.

At the chorus of "YES" that replied, I went down below to get my dinner ready, and quickly, as they were threatening to open a Costco-sized bag of potato chips instead of waiting for the lovely dinner I had prepared.

Chapter Fifteen

"Why haven't I heard anything?"

From the same telephone transcript acquired by Janeva in a later book, she again felt it important and appropriate to add here

Max stared at his computer in frustration. He had just finished an unpleasant call with his investors. They were getting impatient and he had gambled everything on this. Looking at his iPhone for the umpteenth time, he wondered again. Where was the call? Why hadn't he heard from them? He was getting desperate. Time was running out!

He needed that chip and its data. The shareholders' meeting was coming up, and if he didn't deliver the chip his company would be in ruins! He would lose his plane, his luxury homes, of which he had several, his antique car collection. Worse, he might even end up in jail because after the satellite call from Princess Louisa he had told the investors that he would unveil the chip, followed by a quick release of the product.

He knew his competitors were working on a similar product and he had to be first to grab the market share. This was why his investors had given him so much money, this was the product that would revolutionize the industry and lock in the existing consumer base. More importantly, all projections were that this product would convert all the customers for the new product into loyal consumers of his company's existing product suite, taking the company to the next level!

He jumped as his phone rang. Picking it up, he said, "Finally! I'm on my way."

"I don't have it…" came the hesitant and frightened sounding voice.

"What?!" Max roared, "Where is it?"

"I don't know," squeaked the reply.

"You don't know where it is?? You told me you had it!" he yelled into the phone.

"I did, I thought I did, I mean it's missing; I, I think I know where it is," came the mumbled reply.

"Well, if you know where it is, then why don't you have it?" Max demanded.

"Um… well… uh… Perhaps, I think it could be…"

"Perhaps! Don't speculate! Do you or don't you

know where it is?" Max cut in.

"It's, uh, in the…" came the garbled response.

Interrupting, Max yelled, "WHAT?! I don't have time for this, I need that chip NOW! I can't have it showing up from Lorenzo's company. That would be a disaster. Get me that chip today. Understood?!"

"Yes, understood. The yacht Atlantis will be delivered this weekend from Canada, where it's been impounded. I'll get back on it and search the office," said the voice from the other line.

"Damn it, don't screw it up this time! They have increased security at Lorenzo's office after your botched break in," growled Max.

"Yes, I will get it! This time."

"You are lucky you have a second, or should I say third chance. But it's your LAST, and I need that chip today!" Max snarled.

"I won't let you down."

"Be sure you don't. I hate incompetence.… Get this done and clean up your loose ends or you will be the one looking behind you." After a moment's hesitation Max added, with malice, "You're not my only player," and ended the call.

Chapter Sixteen

The Easy Way Out

From Stella's Diary

Back at our waterfront town of Archipelago, Stella Blackwood sat outside Starbucks watching the commuter trains go by. The town was named for the cluster of small islands surrounding it. Over the years many bridges had been built to connect the various islands, crisscrossing the small waterways. The narrower areas had filled in and subsequently developed, so it now felt like one continuous community instead of a collection of separate islands.

Stella glanced down at her grande latte and vanilla scone; they were untouched and she pushed them away. Both were usually her favorites and always cheered her up, but not today. Putting her head in her hands to hide her tears, she subsided into quiet sobs.

John was having an affair with Catherine. When she had finally confronted him last night, he had yelled that he was going to leave her for Catherine. What was she going to do? How would she survive? She had no money of her own, and neither did John. They were not only flat broke but in debt, plus it was her name that was on all the debts. She had trusted him when he said he needed to put the mortgage and other assets in her name to keep them safe, in case his company was sued. That was before the mortgage crisis and the recession that had followed it. They had walked away from their home in foreclosure when they couldn't refinance because the housing market had collapsed, so that their beautiful home was worth only a quarter of what they had purchased it for only a few years before.

Losing the house might not have been so bad if John hadn't borrowed against in with second and third loans, all in her name. And the slimy people he had borrowed from were not as accommodating as the bank. They had no intention of writing the debt off as a bad debt: they expected to be paid back in full with interest—a huge amount of interest!

Her life with John had started off so well, she thought, as she stared out at a passing commuter train. She had been a hair stylist in Silicon Valley before the recession, in those wonderful days when companies regularly seemed to be going public with huge IPOs, and there was easy money to be made. John had used his small inheritance from his grandfather and started up a venture capital company. She would listen and ask careful and skillful questions of the swanky CEO wives who frequented the hair salon and spa she worked at, and pass the information on to John. Those were the best days....

Oh, and she had been talented also, back in the day, on track to becoming a senior hair designer. Truly it's amazing what women will say when you are doing their hair or nails. She would bring home all the juicy gossip she had heard during the day, and John would act on it, either by investing in the new startup or buying that company's shares. It was so easy to learn about a big product announcement or a merger or a husband doing the pre-IPO dog and pony show. They had made so much money! Enough that John's small company had eventually moved to Wall Street.

She had missed California very much, but the excitement of New York was exciting, invigorating. Still, it was the sun that she missed. The cold winter and hot humid summer days were not to her liking. She sighed. Yes, it's good to be back on the West Coast, even if it is just for a short time, she thought, lifting her face to the warm sun and endless blue sky.

She almost smiled. Then the reality of John leaving her came crashing down on her again and tears started to run down her face. A young boy and his mother walked by on their way into the Starbucks, and she heard the boy say to his mother, "That lady needs a hug, Mommy." Quickly wiping away her tears, Stella again thought, What I am going to do? Then she fell back into her memories of better days, parties in New York, with her stylish new wardrobe, when she had become one of the swanky wives herself. But she still brought home the gossip and so was helpful to John, so he encouraged her to go to volunteer luncheons and the spa, etc. In those setting, too, women didn't realize how much intel they gave away if you knew what to ask and could read between the lines.

But that was before, before the big property developments that collapsed. Then there was the desperate pyramid scheme that was going to save them and that didn't work out so well—oh, and now the IRS was after them.... Putting her head back in her hands, Stella couldn't even process those implications. She was sure that John had cheated on his taxes for many years, that was his way, always chasing after easy money. Regrettably, she had followed him every step of the way. It's amazing what charm and looks can do.... Shaking her head she realized that John wasn't leaving her, he was just following the most direct path to money, and that was Catherine, the rich widow.

Why had she been so trusting? She knew what he was like. She had seen him swindle and scam other people; he was proud of it. Anything that made him easy money! Standing up and walking toward the commuter train platform she thought, If only Catherine wasn't in the picture, then I could have my life back....

She was walking down the paved platform with the crowd as the long commuter train was pulling up when she was pushed from behind. Stella flew through the air in front of the slow-moving but unstoppable train.

Chapter Seventeen

"You will do it!"

Trent's contribution

If you happened to find yourself in the Braise-Bottoms' elegant home at 8 am on a sunny September morning, you would probably expect to see Trent and Wiffy sitting amiably sipping coffee in the breakfast room off the kitchen as they perused the newspaper and nibbled on some soft-boiled eggs and toast, exchanging polite conversation like "At my committee meeting today…" or "Should we attend that charity fundraiser on the tenth?"

What was actually being said would surprise you. In stark contrast to the perfect symmetry of a home clearly decorated entirely by an interior designer with excellent taste, complete with fresh-cut flowers, knick-knacks, and books all perfectly arranged in what could be an Ethan Allan showroom, you would hear the sounds of yelling—from Wiffy! She no longer looked like a meek, washed-out lady who spent her days at charity luncheons, smiling and speaking in quiet, modulated tones. Wiffy was yelling in a harsh voice, "Don't shake your head at me! You will find me those shoes!"

"But, but I don't know where they are…," replied Trent, weakly.

"You had better figure it out! This is all your GOD DAMN FAULT in the first place! You brought me the wrong shoes!!!"

"I don't understand! What is the big deal? They look exactly like your white boat shoes and they fit you, don't they?"

"Well, they're not mine!" yelled Wiffy, waving a large kitchen knife in Trent's face.

Backing away until he ran into the fridge, Trent stammered "How... h h how?"

"Look, Einstein, if I don't have the shoes, then one of the other women who were there does," Wiffy pointed out, rolling her eyes. "The obvious person is Stella. Just go and get them from her."

"I can't just show up uninvited at her house and demand her shoes," Trent managed to stammer as he tried unsuccessfully to push himself into the fridge.

"And why not? What about the others? Have you checked their boats and houses?" growled Wiffy, drawing the knifepoint down Trent's Adam's apple.

"Unh uh."

"Then I think it's high time you did something! I didn't sacrifice everything to be blocked by the likes of you!" This was delivered in barely a whisper, with the knifepoint now pricking the skin.

This had happened many times before, the knife pricks always small, easily explained away as shaving cuts. And as in the past, Trent knew this was his opening. If he could get her venting about past wrongs, he could escape further threats with the knife. Besides, he needed to find John to get to Stella. He said quietly, "I don't know what you are talking about.... You have a good life."

"A good life, a good life!" she bellowed. "I gave up my career for what—what, I'd like to know?!" Answering her own question she sneered, "Because Braise-Bottoms don't work. But who, I ask, took your small inheritance and tripled it? ME!" She waved the knife in the air to make her point and backed away to continue her diatribe as she paced around the kitchen's granite-topped island. Breathing a sigh of relief, Trent put his finger to the small cut on his neck to stop the bleeding.

"It was my connections, me, me, me! That's what got us the money to buy this house!" she yelled, waving the knife around like a pointer. "I can't believe I let YOUR mother pressure me into giving up my job—I was on the fast track as one of the few female electrical engineers back then.... And MY parents gave up so much so I could get a decent education and a great job at a growing company. Look at that company today—it's huge, and I would be a senior vice president by now. By the time that controlling old bat your mother dies, we will be too old to enjoy the money! All those years I lost not working, being a slave to you and the children,... using my connections to invest that pittance of a fortune you inherited to make enough money so we could have a nice house, boat, and vacations, pay for those bratty kids of ours to go to prep schools and expensive colleges...." And so it went.

Trent, having heard this all many times before, had edged over to the breakfast nook and was quietly sipping his coffee as he pretended to give Wiffy his complete attention. In fact he was contemplating how he might explain to John that he needed Stella's white boat shoes. If he didn't get the damn shoes.... His dominating mother would no doubt side with Wiffy. The two women were usually like oil and water, except on the rare occasion when she would surprisingly side with his awful wife. What was with the shoes, anyway? He was startled out of his thoughts by Wiffy's final burst of anger.

"Get going! What's the goddamn holdup?" she screamed, now standing on her tippy toes and still waving the knife in Trent's direction.

Chapter Eighteen

Romancing Catherine

Catherine's narrative

Catherine sat in a quiet corner of the Yacht Club deck. She had spent the previous day, Saturday, at the company. Everyone at the company had to work that Saturday to get the new product launched, and to her surprise she had really enjoyed herself. Having never worked in an office before, she hadn't known what to expect. After graduating from high school she had been sent for a year of finishing school in Switzerland and had then been admitted to Yale, where she had gotten a degree in art history and met Lorenzo. Lorenzo hadn't wanted her to work so she had spent her days painting in the studio in their home and gardening.

But working at the company felt like it was just what she needed; with so much to learn, she was sure the days would just fly by. When she'd returned home the night before from the office, she'd been so tired she'd fallen straight into bed and had the first good night's sleep since Lorenzo's death. John and Stella were still at the house, and this was surprising, as the funeral had long since passed. But Stella was a good cook and Catherine enjoyed the company. She wasn't looking forward to the day they would leave and the house would be empty.

Yesterday had been an especially good day. She had worked with the marketing group and had surprised everyone with her artistic skills as she quickly sketched graphics for the web design and other marketing material. It felt great.

Ordering a latte, she looked at her watch and wondered why John had wanted to meet her at the Yacht Club for Sunday brunch and not at the house. A soft touch on her shoulder made her jump, and she looked up to see John standing behind her. He gave her one of those seductive smiles and sat down beside her. Smiling back—how could she not?—she asked, "Where is Stella?"

"She won't be join us...." He looked up as the waiter appeared and ordered a 12-year-old single malt scotch, then continued in a purring voice, "I haven't seen her today, but I expect she is packing."

Catherine's face fell. "Oh... are you leaving then? Going home to New York?" she said sadly.

John reached out, taking her hand. Leaning forward, he looked into her eyes and spoke so quietly that Catherine, who was still processing his closeness and trying to decide how to react to his holding her hand, had to lean forward to hear him.

Fortunately, at that moment the waiter appeared with John's drink and a chit for him to sign. To make it easy for members, the Yacht Club used a chit system, meaning that members signed for what they consumed at the club and were then billed monthly. Since John was not a member, Catherine had to extract her hand from his grip in order to reach for the chit and sign her name and member number.

John took the opportunity to order Eggs Benedict for two and a vintage bottle of champagne. Catherine looked up in surprise; she didn't even like hollandaise sauce and always ordered it on the side. But as she loved champagne and actually felt like celebrating after her successful day at the company, she decided to let it go. So far, John and Stella hadn't offered to pay for anything, though they'd been her houseguests for several weeks. But in truth she hadn't asked them to because she was happy to have their company and Stella's cooking. She herself had never been much of a cook, though she had prepared meals for Lorenzo and her father for years; keeping house for Lorenzo had been her life, and with him gone she no longer had the heart to do it. The soft pop of the champagne cork followed by the bubbling sound of champagne being poured pulled Catherine's thoughts back to the table and

John.

"To the future," he said, as he handed her a glass.

After the toast John asked about the company. Catherine shared details about the new product and launch. John's skilled questioning, combined with her new enthusiasm for working led her to talk and talk. She knew she was telling him confidential company information, but the champagne on her empty stomach removed any barriers she should have had, and soon John had moved to sit beside her on the bench seat. As the bottle emptied, Catherine floated on a champagne glow—and on the surprising feelings and heat she felt now every time John touched her. This was becoming more and more frequent, and she was having confusing, disjointed thoughts that seemed to alternate between Where is our food? and I wonder what it would be like to kiss John?

With the perfect timing of a charmer, John saw his opportunity, waved the waiter with the food away, put his arm around Catherine, and said, "It looks like the Atlantis has just arrived, and I think it's only proper that we go down to the dock to greet her."

This seemed reasonable to Catherine, who was now more than a bit tipsy and ready to go anywhere with John. With his arm around her, they made their way down the ramp and dock to the Atlantis. Boarding the yacht, they were greeted by the crew. Catherine gave them a crooked smile as she struggled to remember what it was she wanted to ask Carl the first mate and his girlfriend Sandy. It had something to do with Lorenzo's murder, she was sure of that, but what was it? She knew the Canadian Police had cleared them because the detective in charge had called her frequently in the past few weeks with more and more questions.

John was relieved to see that the crew had their bags packed and were keen to depart for their long-overdue shore leave with friends and family. Though Catherine had been planning, pre champagne, to tell them that the yacht was for sale and talk to them about the opportunity of working for the new owner, she forgot all about it because she was still trying to remember what she wanted to ask Carl and Sandy. She had, however, come prepared with their pay envelopes in her purse. But in her current state all she could manage was a silly smile as she handed out the envelopes.

John took charge, slapping the first mate on the back and promising to call them with the new schedule. In a moment of clarity Catherine realized how inappropriate it was that she was drunk, hanging on her dead husband's friend's arm, smiling up at him like a school girl in love, but she couldn't help it. It felt good, and she wanted to kiss John. Fortunately you don't last long as yacht crew if you are particularly sensitive to virtue, and they all left smiling and shaking their heads at the antics of the rich.

John closed and bolted the sliding door, then turned crossed the few steps to the bar where Catherine was trying to open yet another bottle of champagne.

Taking the champagne from her, he wrapped his arms around her and kissed her passionately. In a scene reminiscent of a James Bond movie, they moved together to the master stateroom, tearing each other's clothes off as they went.

Afterward, Catherine stretched like a cat, picked up her glass of champagne, and snuggled into John's chest, thinking to herself that it had felt good, and she felt good. John's lovemaking was so different from Lorenzo's, so passionate. She had been married to Lorenzo for so long she had forgotten what it was like to feel desirable.

John raised his glass to hers: "To many yachting trips together on the good ship Atlantis."

"Mmmm," she said. "John, you do know that I'm selling the yacht."

"Yes, you might have mentioned that, but I'm sure I can change your mind. You did make that decision immediately after Lorenzo died."

"You are, of course, correct, and after this afternoon my memories of this yacht are much improved, but I really must sell," replied Catherine.

"Must sell?" inquired John.

"Yes. Unfortunately, I need the money," Catherine explained.

"No...." said John in disbelief, seeing her face he said

"If you need the money, then sell the company, not this lovely yacht."

"Oh John,... it's complicated."

"Try me, Catherine... I'm one hundred percent here for you. Let me fix all your problems. Let us keep the yacht. Don't worry—I will arrange all the upkeep and I will be the captain; just think of all the great places we cave visit... I know: let's ship the yacht to Caribbean for the winter, then to the Mediterranean for the summer. It will be wonderful, so romantic: here's to tropical nights." He raised his glass and toasted her again.

Shocked and very confused by the direction the conversation had taken, Catherine said, "Umm, John, I'm not sure what you are talking about, but I really must sell the yacht."

"Oh, okay, I get it: too many memories. So sell the Atlantis and we will buy a new yacht just for us and start fresh, making new memories together," John said in his silky voice, snuggling into her in that manner that had worked so well for him in the past.

"Us, together?" Catherine said, as she tried to pull herself away from John. "John, what are you talking about? What about Stella? You are married!"

"Stella left me," said John sadly. "We haven't been close for years and once we—" he leaned over and caressed and kissed her neck to make sure she knew the "we" he was talking about was the two of them "—started spending so much time together, I knew—and more importantly she knew—that it was over. Stella and I had a big fight last night and she left this morning.... Yes, she up and left. She said she was leaving me and going to move back to her home town. I slept in your second guest room last night, and when I got up she had packed up all her things and was gone."

"Oh John, I'm so sorry; I'm sure she will be back. All couples have fights."

With a sudden flash of anger John snapped back, "NO. Aren't you listening? We haven't been a married couple for years! Do I have to spell it out for you? We don't love each other anymore; actually, I think it would be a stretch to say we even like each other. We don't have kids," Taking a deep breath he continued, this time quietly, "so there is nothing to keep us together, especially now that she knows that I love you."

"But John... " was all she could think to say.

"I know you need time to adjust. Don't worry, my darling, we will go slowly." He moved very close to her and very gently brushed his lips against hers. Then before she could object he pulled away and lifted his champagne glass in a toast: "To new beginnings."

"No, John!" Catherine said forcefully. Then seeing his devastated look, similar to that of a child who has been told No by a cherished adult, she continued in a soothing voice. "John, that does sound lovely, but I can neither afford nor do I desire to spend months on end on this yacht or any other yacht."

"What do you mean?" demanded John. "You love boating as do I! It's one of the many things that we have in common."

"Things, things in common" Catherine stuttered. "But John, I really don't like boating. I never have! It was Lorenzo's passion, and I only did it for him. Most of the time I was seasick... I know people thought I was hung over, but the medication made me sleepy."

Looking rather stunned, John slowly rallied with "Uh, well, that's a real shock and very disappointing! Mmmm; okay, then, it's a second home.... Should it be a condo on the Med? I've always loved Cassis, no, St. Tropez Would be better! Yes, that's it. And we will buy a day boat for me to bomb around in and visit the other yachts."

"John!" snapped Catherine, interrupting his dream. "To be clear, Lorenzo spent all our money on the company. I can't afford a second home anywhere, particularly the Med. I don't even know if I can afford the house I live in."

"You—YOU have no money?" said John very slowly, enunciating every word carefully. He looked very pale and sick as the blood drained from his face.

"John, John—are you okay? Here, I'll get you some water to drink," Catherine said, jumping out of bed to match her actions with her words.

Taking a big breath and exhaling slowly, John leaned forward and said under his breath, "Sell the company, it's a start.... Sell the company, yacht, house,... it might be enough." Grabbing Catherine's arm as she moved from the bed and looking her in the eye, he declared, "I have a buyer for the company."

"But John, I can't sell, I don't want to sell, I won't sell! I'm enjoying working at the company."

"Listen, Catherine, I appreciate that you are having FUN playing at working, but that's not who you are."

"Who I am…" repeated Catherine, feeling like a foolish parrot but too stunned to think of anything more intelligent to say.

"Yes. You are a beautiful and gracious wife, you were born and bred to support your husband. Your work is to host parties, remember names, and send thank you notes. Work, NO! You WILL sell that company, this yacht, and house, then we WILL get married. We'll have enough money from selling everything to move into one of those new luxury suites they just finished across the bay. With your contacts and my savvy investment strategy, we will be back on top in no time." Reaching over and grabbing her by the back of her hair, he gently but firmly pulled her into a long kiss that she tried to struggle out of, but the harder she did the more pressure he used. Finally he broke off the kiss and continued:

"Now be a good girl, and let's agree to sell the company so we can continue this pleasant celebration." The last was said in a horse voice that sent shivers through Catherine.

Desperately she said, "John… I don't want to sell the company and I don't want to marry you!"

John calmly said, "Yes, you do." He grabbed her by the arm and yanked her out of the bed. Then, pushing her in front of him, down the stairs to the engine room, he added, "Either you change your mind or you can join Lorenzo."

Chapter Nineteen

"Why didn't you tell me?"

We woke up docked at Geranium Island on Sunday to a cool foggy morning—great for joggers, dog walkers, and gardeners, but I wanted to sit on the deck enjoying my coffee and newspaper in the sun. This is a real treat because at home I get all my news online, and I really do enjoy the old-fashioned newspaper. It's great to see a whole page at a glance, and I love the folding challenge, followed by finding the right page to continue the article, then refolding the paper—not to mention my favorite part, the page negotiation with Thomas. We were mid-debate about who should have page A5 when my cell phone rang. Since my phone was down below in the galley, I reluctantly handed page A5 to a gloating Thomas and went to see who was calling me on Sunday morning.

"Hi, Janeva," came Tiffany's voice across the cell line.

"Tiff. What's up?"

"Well, you know we always go to visit Cody's aunt after church on Sundays."

"Yes... is she okay?"

"Oh, yes, she is still the same; the cancer isn't getting worse but she seems thinner and getting depressed. I guess being in a hospital day after day gets you down. But that's not why I called: as we were leaving I saw Stella Blackwood on a stretcher in the hall."

"Stella? Really?! How did you know it was her? Have you met her?" I asked surprised.

"No—I mean yes, I've seen her at the club. It's her; I checked the name on her chart. I know I haven't met her before but we recognized her from the Yacht Club fundraiser, when you and Thomas sat with her, so I knew she was a friend of yours. That's why I'm calling."

"Thank you, Tiffany, it was good of you to call me," I replied. "Do you know why Stella was in hospital?"

"Not for sure, it's all confusing. She was in bad shape.... " Taking a deep breath Tiffany continued, "She was very bruised, swollen and bloody. She was waiting to go in for full body x-rays because they say she has multiple broken bones."

"Oh my God, how horrible! Was she in a car

accident?" I asked.

"No, that's the confusing part: the aid who was pushing her around said under her breath that she had JUMPED in front of the commuter train. She is on suicide watch and they are searching for relatives to advise on what facility to send her to once she is all bandaged up."

"She jumped in front of a train! Wow, I don't believe it, really? I hardly know her, but from what I know it's not in character! Where is John—her husband?" I added, in case Tiffany didn't know his name.

"I asked if they had located her husband and was told no, not yet, and that they would appreciate any assistance I might be able to give."

"Right; that's where I come in," I replied. "I know they were staying with Catherine after Lorenzo's death anyway... hmm. They may still be. I'll call over there now. If I don't find him there I'll try Trent Braise-Bottom the Third; he might know where I can reach John." Even with this sad news, I still had to work hard to stifle the giggle that always came when I said Trent's ridiculous name.

"Janeva, that's not all." Tiffany added. I resisted filling in the silence as I sensed that something else was bothering her. "It's just that when I took Stella's hand and told her I was a friend of yours and you would be able to track down her husband.... Oh, this is so strange... maybe she was delirious with pain killers..."

"Tiffany, what did she say?" I interrupted.

"That John pushed her"!

"What... what exactly did she say?" I insisted.

"I quote, 'No, not John, he pushed me... John pushed me.' Then she started to cough up blood and the aid waved me away."

Thanking Tiffany and ending the call, I called Catherine's house and left a voice message. Then I called Trent's and left the same message. I easily retrieved those phone numbers from the Yacht Club member directory we keep on our boat. Catherine's cell number was on my cell phone contact list from the stabbing at Lorenzo's office on Friday. Again no answer, so I left yet another voice message, then called the club to see if Catherine, Trent, or John were there and was told that Catherine and a guest had lunched in the lounge but had left a little while before.

I asked to be transferred to the upstairs lounge where they had eaten and was told by the bartender, after he looked out the window, that they were walking down the dock to the Atlantis, that yacht having just returned to the dock from Canada. Unsure what to do next, I decided to bring Thomas up to speed and get his ever practical advice.

"Don't stress about it. I'm sure the hospital will find John soon enough; anyway, it sounds like Stella might need some time to sort things out first," was Thomas's reply after I relayed the events to him.

Then, looking at his watch, Thomas announced, "Time to leave." I knew this meant "I'm going to start the engine now and cast off the lines," so I said a quick goodbye to Greg and Steph. Kevin and Sam hadn't emerged from their boat and the shades were still down, so either they were still asleep or they were watching a movie or deep in a video game.

As I'd predicted, our engine was already running by the time I had said my goodbye, so I untied our bowline and tossed it on the boat, then moved to the mid-ship line and waited for Thomas to release the stern line. After uncleating the mid-ship line and giving the boat a big push, I jumped on.

Fortunately for me there was no wind, as the phone call from Tiffany had distracted me and I hadn't finished stowing away all the breakfast dishes. After I finished coiling the dock lines and putting them in the hatch, along with the fenders, I went down below to finish up with the dishes and remind Katie that she had better get packed up now because her friend Alix's mom was picking her up at the Yacht Club as soon as we arrived; the girls were going to Alix's house to work on their school project.

Leaving Katie doing packing, I joined Thomas on deck; it was a quiet peaceful morning as we sat companionably watching the fog burn off, to be replaced by sun and a cloudless blue sky.

"I just can't believe the luck Catherine is having," I said.

"Luck has nothing to do with it! She just made poor choices in friends," Thomas replied with an eye roll.

"What? Just because her husband was murdered and John's wife was pushed or jumped in front of a commuter train?" I asked, incredulous.

"Yes," replied Thomas, who hates to analyze other people. Ignoring him, I carried on, hoping that I might draw him in and get his insights. "And how do you explain the break-in at the company and stabbing of the security guard... now, that had nothing to do with choices that Catherine made."

"True, that is very strange. I don't understand why she doesn't just sell that company. She should take her money and get away from that group."

"Oh, I forgot to tell you! She can't sell even if she wanted to."

"What why on earth not?" Thomas demanded.

"Because Lorenzo needed money to finish some new product he was about to launch." I paused. "He was counting on investor financing that was to close last week, but with his death it all fell apart."

"So all the more reason to sell. It does seem like the obvious solution."

"It might, but he put the house up for a line of credit that is now maxed out. I gather the only way they will make payroll and the office lease payment is from the sale of the Atlantis on Monday."

"Okay, okay, but I still don't get it. If she sells the company, the new buyer deals with the line of credit in the purchase. Catherine gets the lien off her house, which by the way she should sell, too, and start a new life. Really, what am I missing?"

"When you put it that way, its seems very clear, but

Frank—"

"Who is Frank?" Thomas interrupted.

"Frank Duffy is the company COO and acting CEO. He said that the other company's offer was way too low, especially since the new product was about to launch. I've seen some of it and it's amazing." I went on to tell him about it and showed him the Dexia app and told him about the new product. Of course I made him promise not to tell anyone. "So you see, a purchaser will have to pay a lot more once the new product—E-lett something or other— is selling. Catherine wants to wait to sell, plus I think she is doing it as much to honor Lorenzo's dream as for the money." Looking at the horizon where the grey-blue water met the clear, light-blue sky, my thoughts returned to Lorenzo's murder.

"It's a good thing that the Canadian police are convinced that the murderers are those two missing crew members."

"Why do you say that?" Thomas asked.

"Well, with all that's happened to Catherine, if its not them, then it has to be someone we know.... I wonder what Lorenzo did to them that they had to murder him?" I mused.

Laughing, Thomas said, "Sorry. I completely forgot to tell you: that Canadian police inspector called me."

"Really? Was it because they had released the Lorenzo's, I mean Catherine's, yacht?"

"No... they wanted to ask me more questions.

Apparently they found the two missing crew members and ruled them out as suspects."

"What! Really?!" I cried.

"They called..."

I interrupted "But why?

"Because..." Thomas tried again.

"Where were they?"

"They were at..."

"Who else could have done it?"

"Stop with the hundred questions and give me a chance to answer," was Thomas's frustrated reply.

I firmly closed my mouth and looked at him expectantly.

"I'm not going to tell you unless you get me another cup of coffee," he replied with a smirk; he was enjoying taunting me.

"But the Yacht Club is right there," I said, pointing to the Yacht Club and marina on our bow.

"No coffee, no story," was the frustrating reply.

"Okay, okay. Do you want a biscotti with that?" I inquired sarcastically as I headed down below to pour him a coffee out of the thermos I had made earlier.

Stepping up from the galley into the cockpit, I handed Thomas a mug of coffee.

"Were is my biscotti?"

Rolling my eyes, I handed it to him.

"Look there is the Atlantis" I said as we turned into the marina. "Tell me, why were the two crew members released if they murdered Lorenzo? And if they didn't murder Lorenzo, then who did?"

"You're doing it again!"

"Sorry, please tell me!" I begged

"Can't now, we are at our slip."

Groaning, I got up to secure the docking lines to our boat, then yelled for Katie to come and help. I jumped off the boat with my line, securing it to its cleat, then I caught Katie's bow line, secured it, and finally, after a short sprint on the dock from the bow to the stern of our boat, I grabbed the stern line from Thomas. Back on the boat I went down below to finish the cleanup while Thomas grabbed the hose and busily scrubbed the deck.

As the sounds of scrubbing and rinsing subsided, Thomas yelled down "Katie, Alix's mom is here to pick you up!"

Katie grabbed her school knapsack, gave me a quick kiss, and was gone. I smiled to myself and wondered how much work the girls would really get done for their project in a group setting. But I guess it's never too early for them to learn the ninety-ten percent rule. Since Katie was part of the ten percent who do all the work, I was sure to hear about the project in great detail as she vented later that so-and-so wasn't doing his or her share.

Thomas left to walk Katie up the dock to where

Alix and her mom were waiting. As I tossed our overnight bags up onto the deck from below, my gaze strayed to the Atlantis. It looked both familiar to have it back in its slip and strange, since the big yacht's space had been empty for the last few weeks and I was used to seeing open water behind it now.

Turning to go back down below to bring up the next load, I was surprised to see John Blackwood walking down the dock with an overnight bag. How strange! I thought. Oh well—I'd better finish the packing before Thomas returns with the wheelbarrow to move our bags and the cooler to the car.

It only took a minute to finish loading the cooler and lug it up to the deck, where I was even more surprised to see Trent walking up to the Atlantis. What was he doing there?

Chapter Twenty

"Now what?"

My curiosity was piqued, to put it mildly. Why was John hanging out at the club with Catherine when his wife was in hospital needing him, and why was he going to the Atlantis? Just as interesting, why was Trent following him? Looking up the top of the dock, I was happy to see Thomas chatting with some other club member. I wondered if I could get to the Atlantis and back before he returned. I did, after all, have a good reason to go to big Hatteras yacht: someone had make sure that John was told about his wife; he couldn't possibly know or he would be by her hospital bed. Jumping off the boat, I walked quickly to the Atlantis. Thomas would be furious to learn that I was following Trent who was following John when I should be minding my own business and packing up the boat.

Looking back, I was happy to see that Thomas was still deep in conversation and that several other club members had joined him, forming a small circle at the top of the dock. So I quickly darted up the dock that the Atlantis was moored on, relieved that I was now out of Thomas's sight.

I was surprised to see that the dock was empty, with the exception of the small overnight bag that John had been carrying. Looking very out of place, the bag was just sitting in the middle of the dock, and I wondered why John would drop the bag there. The Atlantis was the only boat on this dock, which was the last dock in the marina, so there was nowhere else for him or Trent to go. They had to be on the boat, or else they would have had to walk past me as I made my way here.

My eyes moved again to the overnight bag and then to the yacht. Should I pick up the bag? It would give me another reason for boarding the Atlantis…. If I didn't do something quickly, I might as well go back to our boat. So instead of standing around looking foolish, I picked up the bag, thinking to myself, John must have gotten distracted, talking to Trent perhaps, and put the bag down and forgotten it, so I should just take it to him; I need to tell him about his wife anyway.

Taking a deep breath to steady my nerves, with bag in hand I walked to the stern of the boat and boarded. The boat was quiet, too quiet; where were the crew? I walked up the stairs through the outdoor seating and dining area to the main cockpit sliding glass door and knocked and knocked, but no one came, and when I finally tried the door I was surprised to find it locked. What should I do now? I could see into the main salon and dining area through the sliding glass door, and the rooms were deserted. Now what? Where could they all be? I wondered, as I looked around the marina. All the neighboring boats were buttoned up tight and clearly empty. With a sigh I decided to put the bag on the cockpit table and turned to return to our boat.

It was as I was walking to the table that I heard the bang, followed by a muffled scream—a woman's scream of "Noooo!"—It definitely came from somewhere below. My first thought was Catherine: Was she in trouble again? Still clutching the bag, I turned and ran along the narrow side deck to the side door where the galley was. Darn, locked again!

I continued, circumnavigating the yacht, past the bow lounge seat and back to the cockpit and up the long curved stairway to the pilothouse deck. Finally I found an open hatch. Quickly I went down the inside stairway to the glamorous main deck landing. I decided that the main salon, dining room, and galley were empty, as I had already seen inside those rooms through doors and windows as I ran around the outside of the boat. So I turned in the opposite direction, heading toward the bow and master stateroom. Here I collided with Trent, who was just leaving the master stateroom.

"Trent, what are you doing here?" I stammered.

"Why do you have Wiffy's bag?" Trent wheezed simultaneously, holding his stomach and looking at the bag I was still carrying, which had swung forward and knocked the wind out of him in the collision.

"Wiffy's bag?" I repeated, looking at it. "No, it's John's."

Still breathless, Trent pointed at the dirty and worn embroidery. Looking closely at it, I saw that it was a stylized GB3.

"GB3," I read, and shrugged.

"It stands for 'Georgina Braise-Bottom the Third.' I bought it for her when we were first married."

"Oh, Wiffy's real name is Georgina... I always wondered if she had a real name," was all I could think to say. Then, "It was on the dock, John had the bag.... Why did John have Wiffy's bag? And why are you following him?" I asked, my senses coming back to me.

"I'd better take Wiffy's bag home to her," Trent said, reaching for the bag.

I handed it to him. "Thanks," he said, looking at the bag, puzzled. "I haven't seen this bag for years. Actually I thought it had been given to Goodwill."

"Trent, what are you doing here?" I inquired.

"What are you doing here?" he countered.

"Um, uh, John's wife Stella is in hospital, and I saw him walking down the dock so I thought I should tell him."

"That was nice of you, but I really don't think he

cares." He turned and pointed to the master bedroom scene he had previously been blocking by standing in the small doorway.. A champagne bottle and glasses, messy bedding, and strewn clothes all over the floor told the story.

"But where are they now?" I asked.

Shrugging, Trent said, "I don't know. I was about to up to the pilothouse to see if they were in the hot tub."

"No, they're not, I just came from there," I said, shaking my head. "Anyway, I'm thinking we should just leave, clearly they want to be alone... why else would they have locked all the doors? How did you get in, anyway? The only open door I could find was the pilothouse."

"Locked? No, I came in the main salon door, it wasn't locked, actually it was open partway."

We looked at each other in confusion. "We'd better go," I said.

We turned and walked back down the short hallway and up the stairs to the pilothouse.

"It's locked," I said, trying the hatch door.

"What? Let me try," Trent said, edging past me and handing me back the bag.

After some pushing and shoving I asked, "How did we get locked in? Aren't doors supposed to lock from the inside?"

"Are you sure you came in this way?"

"Yes I'm sure" I snapped.

"Okay, okay, it looks like this hatch locks with a key on the inside and someone has taken the key."

We turned and headed back down the narrow stairs to the main cabin, intending to go out one of the sliding doors on the main floor.

"So why are you here?" I again asked Trent as we were walking.

He shrugged. "Shoes, if you can believe it. I'm looking for a certain pair of shoes—"

"Please don't!" came a faint cry, interrupting Trent.

Trent and I stopped and looked at each other.

"I think that cry came from the lower deck," I whispered.

"What should we do?" Trent said.

"We can't just leave!... Follow me," I said, and continued down the next flight of stairs to the lower deck with the guest cabins and laundry room.

Standing in the small square wood-paneled hallway, we looked around. There were two guest cabins, a laundry and storage room, and then a hallway leading to the bow where Lorenzo's office was located. All the doors were open and the rooms looked empty. I turned and started to walk toward Lorenzo's office in the bow when Trent gently grabbed my shoulder and pointed to the opposite direction, to the stern. We had a silent exchange, and then I shrugged and followed him through a hidden doorway—one I would never have seen, clearly Trent knew this yacht better than I did—then down a narrow passageway to the stern where the large engine room was located.

Trent carefully opened the door and we peeked around it into the dark room. Slowly, I reached around and pushed the light switch on, illuminating a narrow corridor between twin CAT C32 ACERT diesel engines. Seeing nothing unusual, I pushed the light off. We were stepping back out the door when we heard rustling and a muffled sound like "Mmahhmgh." Turning the light on again we ventured into to the room, quietly calling, "Catherine? Are you there?"

Suddenly I felt a shove from behind and I stumbled headlong into Trent, pushing him into the room and hard against the port engine. "What! Ouch!" exclaimed Trent.

"Couldn't you two just leave well enough alone?" came a gruff voice from behind us. Then the lights went out and we heard the door lock.

"Trent, stand still," I whispered.

"Why are you whispering?" he asked. "They know we are here."

"I don't know—because it's so dark, I guess," I replied still whispering.

"Can you find the lights?"

"Yes, I think so. Here, hold the bag so I don't trip on it," I said, pushing the bag in the direction of his voice.

"Ouch, that's my head."

"Sorry." I turned with my arms out stretched and started to slowly feel my way around.

"Wrong way—you almost stuck your finger in my eye," Trent said as I turned around.

I eventually found the door, then the light switch. I have no idea how long it took but it seemed to take hours in the pitch black.

"Thank God," Trent exclaimed, as the lights came on and we tried the door.

"It's locked, of course," I replied, frustrated. "Let's look around, maybe we can find something to help us get out of here."

Trent headed down the short narrow corridor between the engines as I started to look through the compact workbench and toolbox.

"Janeva... remember that sound we heard?"

"Sure," I replied, turning and holding up a tool that looked like it might be useful. "Trent—what's wrong?!" His face was completely white.

"You had better come and see."

Still holding the tool that looked like a big pipe wrench and made me feel safer, I walked toward him.

What I saw made me drop the wrench as both hands went to my mouth to suppress a scream. Catherine was naked and covered in blood, she was gagged and her hands and feet bound with zip ties. How we could have missed her when we first looked in the room was incredible, though it was true that she was curled up in the fetal position in the corner, behind the Genset. But we had almost left her there.

"Is she alive?" I whispered.

Trent reached over to feel her wrist, then he took off her gag "Yes, barely."

"Let's untie her; we have to get out of here," I said.

"Easier said than done. We need scissors or a knife to cut the zip ties," Trent said.

"Scissors... no, I didn't see any of those but I did see a box cutter that should work."

"Now what?" Trent asked me after we had freed Catherine. She was breathing better but was still unconscious. We had torn strips from our clothing to wrap the deep cuts all over her body and slow the bleeding. And I'd wrapped her as best I could in my sweatshirt and some boat rags I had found when I found the pipe wrench, since we needed to keep her warm. "We are still locked in."

"Do you think John did this, or was it the crew?" I asked.

"I'm pretty sure I saw the crew getting into a taxi cab. John and Catherine were already on the boat."

"The whole crew, the same three crew members who were with them in Canada?"

"I think so, but I don't know. Who really looks at staff anyway?"

"It's important Trent. Remember the two who disappeared in Canada? Were they on the boat?

How could they have escaped the RCMP? And come back to finish the job, to finish what they started in Canada when they killed Lorenzo?" I said angrily.

"Sorry. Janeva, I'm pretty sure it was the same three who had been with them in Canada. I really don't know how they slipped past the RCMP—and Customs. You were there, too.... It's not like the Canadian authorities took it lightly. There had to be 20 officers crawling around, plus the Coast Guard scuba divers."

"You're right.... Are you sure that ALL the crew got in the taxi?" I replied with a sigh.

"No, but none of them went back down the dock. I'm sure of that."

"How?" I demanded.

"I had to talk to John about the goddamn shoe or Wiffy would kill me, so when John and Catherine went down the dock I ordered a drink and sat at the window and watched everyone who went up or down the ramp. I saw the crew leave, then a while later I saw John come up the ramp and go to his car and return with a bag." Seeing my raised eyebrows, he added, "I didn't know it was Wiffy's bag. I was too far away to see the monogram."

I couldn't argue with that; the monogram was hard to see even close up. I motioned for him to continue.

"So, seeing my chance, I tried to intercept him on the dock but"—here he looked down at his rounded form and patted his girth—"I wasn't fast enough, so I followed him to the boat."

"What is in that bag, anyway?" I asked.

"Shoes, I hope."

We bent down and unzipped it.

"Looks like nothing but clothes," Trent grumbled. "Still, why did he have Wiffy's bag? Was he having an affair with her, too?! That BASTARD, slimy asshole, F..." the tirade continued. I was astonished to imagined Wiffy, that mousy women who never spoke and seemed to live in the shadows, not only had Trent terrified of her but was sleeping with John!

"We might as well see if there is anything useful in here," I said as I pulled a T- shirt and sweater out of the bag and rolled them up to make a pillow for Catherine's head. Pulling more clothes out I remarked "This is strange. All these clothes are old. And where are the toiletries, deodorant, and shaving stuff?"

"Maybe he planned on using Lorenzo's. It does appear he planned on taking over Lorenzo's life, his yacht, and wife," Trent said as he helped me pull more clothing out of the bag and drape it over Catherine to help keep her warm.

"Look at this." From the zipper compartment on the side of the bag, I pulled out a white shoe—the twin of one I had seen before. "Is this one of the shoes you are looking for?"

Chapter Twenty-One

"Janeva, Janeva!"

Thomas's insisted I add his part of the story here

Thomas, returning to the boat, found Greg, who had just arrived from Geranium Island and was keen to tell Thomas about the sweet dark-blue Hinckley T38R convertible that had taken our spot when we left the island. Listening, Thomas loaded up the bags and food cooler from our boat cockpit and into the wheelbarrow, then headed back up the dock, all the time drilling Greg for details about the Hinckley. After loading the bags in the car they headed back down to Greg and Steph's boat.

"Where is Janeva?" Thomas asked Steph as he entered the cabin of Write-Now, Greg and Steph's cabin cruiser.

"Haven't seen her. If I had to guess I'd say she is still happily bleaching the inside of your boat," joked Steph about Janeva's love of spray bleach to clean.

"Text or call her to come and join us. There's no need to run home—Katie's at a play date, right?" Greg said.

"Greg... it's a study group!" scolded Steph in good humor. "She is too old for play dates now."

"Strange, she's not answering," Thomas said, looking with mild surprised at his phone. "I wonder if her phone ran out of batteries. She loves texting and normally replies instantly."

"You boys stay here and drink your beer. I'll just walk down to your boat and get her," Steph said, leaving the boat and heading down the dock.

~~~~~~~~~~~

Returning a short while later and looking concerned, Steph said, "Thomas, she's not on your boat but her phone and purse are, and yes, before you ask, her phone is on, and no, your text hadn't been picked up."

Greg looking carefully at his wife. "Why the concerned look and tone, Hon? I'm sure she just went looking for Thomas, and is probably wandering around the clubhouse."

"I'm sure you're right.... It's just that she left the Clorox bleach spray, gloves and washcloth out on the counter. It looks like she was partway through cleaning when something caught her attention."

Laughing, Thomas replied, "That wouldn't be the first time—she's easily distracted—but let's go find her anyway; I'm getting hungry."

After checking the docks, parking lot, and the clubhouse, the three stood at the railing of the clubhouse deck looking out over the marina.

"Where could she be?" asked Steph.

"The Atlantis?" replied Thomas.

"Really? Why?" Greg asked, squinting into the setting sun and looking at the Atlantis.

"We got a call from Tiffany on our way over here. Apparently John's wife, Stella, jumped, fell, or was pushed out in front of a commuter train. The hospital staff are looking for John."

"Is she okay?" Steph asked.

Shaking his head, Thomas replied, "Don't know. Tiff said she was confused and disoriented. Humph, the hospital probably just needs to know her insurance coverage details."

"So you think the rumors of John and Catherine having an affair are true, and Janeva went to confront him? That would be highly entertaining and something I would like to witness," laughed Steph.

Thomas and Greg both laughed also at the vision of Janeva scolding John like he was a child.

"It's good to have the Atlantis back in the marina,

the marina seemed empty without her," mused Greg, changing the subject. "They must have caught up with and arrested the missing crew for Lorenzo's murder.... I guess we will never know why they did it," he continued.

Thomas looked up at Greg with a start. "I didn't tell you; I started to tell Janeva..."

"What didn't you tell us?" Greg asked.

"The Canadian police, the RCMP, have called me a several times in the last few weeks."

"Me too! Questions and more questions, as if I didn't tell them everything I knew the first time," Greg agreed.

"They found the two missing crew members and they have been cleared of any wrongdoing. They are foolish, yes, but murders, no. Apparently the first mate, Carl, wanted to propose marriage to his girlfriend, Sandy... remember, she was the housekeeper on the Atlantis. He had this notion that it would be romantic to hike up to the falls and ask her with the falls in the background. They left early that morning, sure that they would be back on the yacht doing their respective jobs well before anyone was up."

Greg and Steph nodded. Then Greg said, "Okay, so what happened to them? We were there all day and they didn't return."

Thomas continued, "You are correct, of course. What the two hadn't counted on was the mud. The heavy rain from the day and night before had made the trail treacherous. Sandy slipped and fell, sliding back down the trail."

"Oh dear, did she hurt herself?" Steph asked, concerned.

"Yes," Thomas continued. "Actually she is very lucky to be alive.... She slid in the mud down an embankment directly toward the falls. Fortunately she got caught up on an outcrop of rock right at the very edge of the falls: she had snagged her shirt on a shrub branch... amazingly lucky for her, a one-in-a-thousand chance. Incredibly, the snag slowed her down enough and so she was able to grab onto a tree just inches from the cliff edge of the falls. Balancing unsteadily on the rock outcrop, she hung on for dear life. Moving ever so slowly and carefully, she eventually managed to get her body wrapped around the tree at her waist, all the time looking down over the cliff, only inches away, at the 100-foot drop. Carl, her boyfriend, was frantic to help her. Now this is where it gets interesting. As she was clawing at the tree, inching her body around it, she lost one of her shoes. The shoe then tumbled down the falls, was caught on the current, and it floated to the dock, where Katie ultimately found it."

"The same shoe we dismantled yesterday on Geranium Island?" Steph put in.

"Yes, the same one, though at the time we didn't realize the importance of the shoe because our boats hadn't been searched, nor had we dismantled the shoe to find the computer chip."

"That makes sense, but how come Carl didn't run down the trail to get help?" Greg asked.

"I asked the police officer the same question.... Apparently as he was trying to crawl down to help her, he also slipped and broke his ankle! Can you believe it?"

"No, well yes,... I can imagine how slippery that trail was. It was a hard, steep climb in places when we climbed it, and that was when it was dry, since the weeks before had been hot and sunny with no rain," Greg commented.

"Didn't it start to rain again during the day?" Steph asked

"You're right. We didn't know it, but the Coast Guard had sent a couple of experienced climbers to look for them as soon as it became clear that the two crew members were missing. I understand that it's not the first time they have had to rescue someone from the falls," Thomas continued.

"So they were okay?" Steph asked.

"Exhausted, cold, hungry, and dehydrated, with many bruises, sprains, and a fracture, but fortunately they didn't get hypothermia. All things considered, they are very lucky."

"So if they didn't murder Lorenzo, then who did?" asked Greg.

Thomas suddenly looked stricken as realization dawned on him "Oh, God," he groaned. "What has she got herself into now? We've got to get over to the Atlantis and make sure Janeva is okay!"

"Thomas! What are you talking about?!" demanded Steph "Why would Janeva need our help on the Atlantis?"

Thomas didn't answer her but instead turned away from the balcony railing they had been leaning on and started hustled through the clubhouse.

"Oh dear, that means it has to be a Yacht Club member... one of us!" cried Steph.

"To quote Janeva's favorites quote by Sherlock Homes "'When you have eliminated the impossible, whatever remains, however improbable, must be the truth.' Since Janeva and the three of us fall into the impossible category, that leaves Catherine, John, Stella, Trent, and Wiffy. And we know at least two of those four are on the Atlantis with Janeva," Thomas said over his shoulder as he hurried down the stairs as quickly as was allowed in the "No running" clubhouse.

Panting to keep up with his speed-walking pace, Steph said, "Oh dear... make that three: I saw Trent following John to the Atlantis when I was putting out the fenders as we were pulling into the marina. I think we can eliminate Wiffy, she is so meek and timid, and Stella is in hospital."

"Steph! Quit analyzing and hurry up," Greg called back to his wife, as he and Thomas started running down the dock to the Atlantis.

Chapter Twenty-Two

"Where is it?"

"Where is the shoe?" Wiffy demanded of John. They were standing in the galley of the Atlantis.

"I don't get it.... I made the switch on the Atlantis when we were in Princess Louisa."

"You screwed it up and I ended up with my shoes, not Stella's."

"Oh, that's why you wanted me to bring a bag down with some clothes and the shoe."

"Bingo! So where is the bag?"

"I left it on the dock, right where you told me to."

"Well it's not there now!"

"They must have taken it."

"Get down to the engine room and check!"

~~~~~~~~~~~~~~~~~~

"Someone is at the door," I said, nudging Trent.

Slowly the door opened, shining in a thin light from the hallway at Trent and me sitting on the floor with the emptied bag open in front of us.

As we sat watching, the door slowly opening, the black muzzle of a gun was the first thing we saw. Then with a bang the door was flung fully opened to reveal Wiffy holding the gun, which she quickly pointed directly at Trent and me. We sat starring at her in stunned silence.

"That shoe! Give it to me now!" Wiffy yelled.

"Why?" I asked clutching the shoe tighter to my chest.

"None of your concern, just give it to me now or..."

"Or?" I said, looking at the gun. "It's not looking too great for us as it is. How much worse can it get?"

Trent elbowed me in the ribs and said, sotto voce, "Shut up!"

"You should listen to him.... He knows what he is talking about. Now hand over that shoe," growled Wiffy.

"If you want the shoe, come and get it," I replied, thinking that Trent and I might have a chance to overpower her.

I was still shocked at the change in Wiffy. She seemed to have grown taller and her eyes now glared at me dark, black and hard. Thinking about it I realized I had never even seen her eyes before; they were always been shyly downcast. But what was even more surprising was Trent's response. He was actually hiding behind me, trembling. "Give her the shoe, Janeva," he whispered urgently.

"NO," I hissed back. "She will kill us."

"Janeva, he knows me well, very, well, you should listen to him," said a calm and amused Wiffy.

"Would you really hurt Trent? He is your husband after all," I replied.

"True, but he is not a very good one; I'm afraid I chose poorly. Now be a good girl and hand over that shoe."

I shook my head.

"Okay, you forced me into it," she muttered, as she reached behind her, grabbing and propelling a surprised John forward into the room.

He looked at us, then back at Wiffy in apparent shock, clearly wondering why he had been suddenly tossed in with us.

"Georgina?" He stammered in surprise.

"Get me that shoe! You moron!" she growled at him.

"Oh," John turned and walked the few steps to me to grab the shoe, but I anticipated him and moved the shoe out of his reach.

I had taken a Kung Fu self-defense classes with Katie a couple years back, and I was pleasantly surprised as it all came back to me. As he tried again to reach the shoe that I had moved behind my back, I stomped on his foot; when he automatically looked down, I karate-chopped him in the neck, at the same time bringing my knee up between his legs; he doubled over, moving his hands down to his crotch, and I poked my fingers in his eyes.

He fell back, crashing into the engine behind him, then crumbled to the ground crying out in pain, one hand clutched to his eyes, the other to his crotch.

I realized that in the fight I had dropped the shoe and turned to see Trent holding it.

"Trent: bring me the shoe," came the command from Wiffy.

"Don't, Trent!" I cried.

To my surprise he looked down at the shoe, then carefully handed it back to me.

Wiffy glared at him. Then shaking her head in disgust, she leveled the gun directly at me.

"As entertaining as this all is, I've had enough. Janeva, give me the shoe."

"Why, you're not going to shoot us, are you?" I said, trying to call her bluff. This turned out to be a mistake.

She arched her eyebrows, then casually moved the gun a slight two inches and fired. Blowing John's head into many, many, pieces... brains, skull, and blood flew everywhere, what a mess. Staring in shock at what had been John's head, all I could think how come in TV and movies it's a clean hole? And Will I ever sleep again? plus My ears are ringing.

Taking advantage of my dazed confusion, Wiffy stepped into the engine room, stepped over John, and grabbed the shoe out of my unresisting, shaking hands. I looked up at her. My senses were slowly starting to come back, especially if I didn't look at the bloody ground or the gore-splattered engine behind me.

Wiffy continued to walk backward toward the door, still keeping the gun leveled at me. Trent was now curled up on the floor fetal style, his hands over his head, whimpering.

"You killed Lorenzo!" I screamed.

"That was regrettable," she replied calmly.

"Why?" Trent asked looking up. The question surprised us all, including Trent himself.

"As you are both dead anyway, I might as well tell you" she boasted.

"Pretty boy John over there—" she laughed a strange strangled laugh as she continued. "He's not so pretty now, is he?"

She waved the gun at him, then said, "Lorenzo was a genius and had come up with a new computer chip that will revolutionize computing as we know it. My job was to get that chip. You see, what makes the chip so valuable is what is saved on it— confidential plans, computer code, and architecture detailing how to mass manufacture and implement the chips itself, plus a new product utilizing the chip technology that will revolutionize the credit card industry.... It was a tricky job because Lorenzo is very careful and kept this chip in a custom flash drive that he plugged into his computer to work on."

"How did you get it? I thought Lorenzo always kept his office door locked," I interrupted.

"Oh aren't you the clever one. You're right on both points. I recruited John to create a distraction so I could get into Lorenzo's office. Of course John was perfectly positioned as he was a guest on the yacht and flirted shamelessly with Catherine when Lorenzo wasn't looking."

"Clever!" I said with admiration... I needed to keep her talking.

"I thought so too. I had John create the distraction by drugging that trophy wife of Lorenzo's. I was the one who went to find Lorenzo in his office to tell him that Catherine needed him, so when Lorenzo ran to help Catherine, I was perfectly positioned to slip in the office and grab the chip." She smiled like a proud mother; clearly she was proud of her plan.

She turned to leave.

"So if you had your chip, why did you kill Lorenzo then?" I asked in a rush. I had to keep her talking, it was my best chance and I refused to give up! Katie was young and she still needed me!!

"He caught me… at his computer... trying to get the chip out of that damn flash drive he had it in…. I had to kill him," she said calmly.

I looked over at Trent, who looked more confused than usual, then turned back to Wiffy, shaking my head and shrugging my shoulders. "I still don't see why you had to kill him—since you had the graphene chip," I ventured.

"Even if I could have talked my way out of being in his office on his computer stealing confidential information, how would I have gotten the computer chip in the shoe?" she replied sarcastically, as though it should have been obvious to me. Then suddenly the light dawned. "WAIT... how did you know the chip was graphene?!" Wiffy yelled in alarm.

Glad my "tactical slip" had done its job, I asked quickly, "What's with the shoes? Very James Bond, but I don't get it. Wouldn't it have been easier to put the computer chip in your pocket?"

A gunshot whizzed past my head, narrowly missing Trent.

I put my hands to my ears; they were ringing with the echo of the gunshot in such a small place. Trent curled himself back into a small ball.

"The shoe was Stella's, one of a pair that were a gift to her from John. I had them specially designed to hide the computer chip so that she would unwittingly carry it through Customs. Then John would exchange the shoes with mine and I would extract the chip so I could deliver it to Max."

"Who is Max?"

"Damn!" Wiffy yelled. "I shouldn't have said his

name—but no matter, you're dead anyway," she said, laughing that crazy evil laugh again.

"But what went wrong?" I said quickly, still stalling for time.

"Oh you are one for details, aren't you?" She smiled a cruel smile at Trent, and then to him she said, "Men, that's the problem: MEN! John gave me the wrong shoe! Really! I know he was holding out for more money.... Foolish man: you see what happens when you cross Max." She pointed her gun at John's mangled head. "But now I have the right shoe and all is well." Here she lifted the shoe up for us to see.

"But why? Why are you stealing computer chips and shoes? I don't understand," Trent asked quietly.

"Didn't you every wonder where the money came?" It was clearly a rhetorical question, so neither Trent nor I answered.

Wiffy continued. "I refused to live groveling to your mother for every penny... so I started using your connections to steal corporate secrets for Max. He pays very well indeed." She laughed a manic sort of laugh that sent shivers down my spine.

Looking at her watch she suddenly snapped, "Enough talk!!"

Shaking my head, not sure how I should respond but knowing that Thomas would find me if I just kept her talking, I asked, "So now that you've told us everything... are you going to shoot us now?" I was surprised at how calm my voice was.

Wiffy smiled and said "No," pointing the gun at us and smiling with only her lips. The effect was to crinkle up her glaring eyes, making her look totally crazy. "I can't leave any evidence this time. When you two idiots were running around the boat I was installing a bomb. It's hidden deep in the bilge. Ha ha," she laughed, in a creepy, insane sort of way, then continued, "I'm going to trigger the bomb with my cell phone... in just a few minutes, ah yes, I will be sitting on the clubhouse deck enjoying a nice glass of Chardonnay, waiting for my sweet husband to join me, when this lovely yacht blows."

Squealing an evil, deranged sort of squeal, that came out like Eeeee, she added, "Of course he can't join me as he's is trapped on this death yacht with you."

Staring at us, she giggled a schoolgirl giggle that was even scarier than the gun and said, "What a field day the club gossips will have trying to piece together what you four were doing on the boat when it exploded. Catherine was having an affair with John; everyone's guessed that, but was the perfect Janeva sleeping with John too, or with Trent? Or were they having a ménage a quatre? For your sake I hope you didn't draw Trent, he is such a bore in bed; John on the other hand was... mmmm, quite lovely. It's such a shame that he had to go and fall for Catherine; can you believe he really wanted to marry her? So much so that he pushed his wife in front of a train so he could be free. Agggg, men are such fools. Look at the time; I must go now. Ta ta."

"They will catch you, you will be the first person

they investigate after the bomb," I said defiantly—
anything just to keep her talking.

"Sorry to disappoint, but I've been very careful;
every indication will point to this being a accident
caused by a generator fuel leak. I know how to do
these things, I am an engineer after all.... It's so sad
for you that you had to get involved. Such is life,"
she finished with a smile, and then slammed the
door shut.

I was moving before the door closed, in a desperate
last-ditch effort to get to it before she locked it, but
as I first had to step over Trent, and then nearly
slipped on some blood as I jumped over John's
body, I was too late.

~~~~~~~~~~~~~~~~~~~

"Janeva, Janeva!" Thomas banged on the locked
sliding-glass cockpit door of the Atlantis. "Steph,
keep banging on the door; Greg, you go up to the
fly bridge, and I'll try the side doors."

The three met again on the aft deck. "All locked,"
said Greg.

"Maybe Janeva is not on the boat?" Steph inquired.

Then they heard the gunshot.

"What was that?" Steph asked, "It sounded like…"

"A gunshot," Thomas and Greg said
simultaneously.

"Break the glass," Greg suggested. Looking for
something strong enough, he picked up one of the

deck chairs and threw it at the glass door. The chair broke into pieces but the glass didn't break.

"Shit, it's marine-grade glass, made to survive storms and crashing through waves. Most yacht owners keep a spare key," Thomas said, looked around him. "Where would Lorenzo keep his?

"Hanging plant? No. Under the seat? No. Bar fridge? Locked under propane heater? No. Tucked in the hand of the Italian sculpture? YES!"

Opening the door, the three ran into the yacht. "Let's split up," Greg suggested.

"All that's left of this floor is the main cabin and media room. Steph, you and Greg go there, then meet me on the lower level!" yelled Thomas as he ran toward the stairway mid ship.

Five minutes later the three stood in the small lower-level landing, having searched all the cabins. "What's left?" Steph asked.

"Engine room and crew quarters," Greg said, pointing aft. Thomas ran through the yacht to the engine room door and wrenched at it.

"Damn, it's locked too."

"Can't we break it down?" Steph asked.

Thomas and Greg both turned to stare at her incredulously. "NO! Its reinforced fireproof steel with soundproofing insulation on the inside," Thomas moaned in frustration. Then, "There will be a key on the bridge," and he ran off.

"We'll check the crew quarters," Greg yelled after

him as he grabbed Steph's arm, dragging her after him.

The crew quarters were unlocked and vacant, so that left only the locked engine room. Greg and Steph had each looked in one of the two crew rooms, then together the small crew galley, then turned and ran back to the engine room.

"You found a key," Greg said unnecessarily, as Thomas worked to put the key in the lock. Opening the door they were stunned by the horrific gory scene that met them.

"Thomas," Janeva cried and ran into his arms.

"What happened?" he asked.

"Later! We need to get off this boat: it's going to explode!" Janeva yelled, turning to go back and grab at Catherine, who was still unconscious. "Help me!" she cried, and instantly the spell was broken as Thomas and Greg ran into the crowded room, pushed Trent out the door and into Steph's arms, then together lifted Catherine between them. Janeva helped pull Trent to his feet and she and Steph dragged him off the boat to the dock.

"NO!!! Don't stop! Keep going—Go, Go, Go!" Janeva yelled to Greg and Thomas, who had been about to put Catherine down to ascertain her injuries.

"She needs medical attention," Greg was saying, "and is anyone else on board? What about the crew?"

"She will need more, as will you, when this boat blows up beside you!" Janeva yelled back at him from the end of the dock. Exchanging a look that said That's a bit far-fetched, but then again, John's head has been blown off, "Better do as she says!" Thomas directed, and together he and Greg grabbed up Catherine's limp body and ran after Janeva, Steph, and Trent.

"No one else is on the yacht, the crew left by taxi. NOW RUN!" Janeva screamed at Thomas and Greg. "Faster!"

BOOM!

The boat exploded, as predicted, throwing all six to the dock.

Some time later, after the firefighters had arrived first on the scene, and the ambulance had taken Catherine to hospital and treated the rest of us for shock, we were interviewed by the police.

"Oh, hi," I said, looking up to see detective Luke Smythe, the same young policeman I'd met after the break-in and fatal stabbing at Lorenzo's office on Friday. Today was Sunday. Was that only two days ago? So much had happened.

He motioned for me to take a seat; we had been whisked off to police headquarters for hours and hours of interviews. There was so much to tell. Fortunately, Detective Luke Smythe was a thorough and diligent detective, so after the break-in at

Lorenzo's office he had contacted the Canadian police to verify Catherine's and my Princess Louisa murder story.

"Did you find Wiffy... I mean, Georgina? Has she been arrested? She said she was going to trigger the bomb from the Yacht Club deck," I asked as soon as they finally stopped drilling me.

"We have searched the area and have a APB out for her arrest. She must be hiding out somewhere. Your husband and Greg Writeman are convinced that she couldn't have escaped from the yacht when they were on board."

~~~~~~~~~~~~~~~~~~~

A week later, late at night on the Carleton Bridge, two figures walked unnoticed along the pedestrian sidewalk of the bridge. The usual steady flow of vehicles had subsided to a car every few minutes, plus the bridge was connected only to a small island that housed many small residential houses whose owners were asleep.

"What rock have you been hiding under?" Max asked.

"Oh I have my bolt holes, here and there," Wiffy replied.

"You think because you finally blew up the yacht that you finished the job?" Max inquired of Wiffy, who had been looking pleased with herself.

"Yes, of course; they are all dead."

"Did you stick around to see?"

"No, there wasn't time; I had to jump off the boat into the disgusting marina water, I swam to shore, triggered the bomb, then I went home to shower. I was freezing!" She shivered at the memory. "But I left the shoe with the flash drive in it for you in your club locker, as we agreed before I left."

"Catherine survived, they all survived," snarled Max.

"Fuck me! Okay, I will take care of her and the rest."

"It was the wrong shoe!"

"WHAT! NO! Damn it! I didn't have time to check the shoe!" Wiffy stammered, looking frightened. "What did you do? What happened?"

"You made my life very, very difficult! Fortunately, I've been manipulating my board of directors for years and was able to buy myself some time to fix some 'bugs' that had come up in development. But I NEED that chip," hissed Max. "Where is the chip, Georgina?" he growled.

"I, I think that bitch Janeva might have it... she knew it was graphene."

Shaking his head, Max asked her softly, "What is that over there?" Then, as Wiffy leaned in to hear him, he took a quick look around to ensure that no one was in sight and dropped his keys. As he bent down to pick them up, he instead grabbed Wiffy's legs and casually but quickly propelled her over the bridge. Not into the water, where there might have been a chance she could survive, but over the concrete. Max picked up his keys and was already moving off the bridge before she crashed down to the concrete below. This bridge was notorious for its suicides, and clearly Wiffy had had all the reason in the world to kill herself.

EPILOGUE ❖

Life Goes On

Recovering in hospital, Catherine found she was drawn to Stella's bedside. The two women spent many hours talking together and found that their memories of John formed an unlikely and unexpected bond between them.

Between collecting the yacht insurance on the Atlantis and, after the product launch, selling Dexia to one of Max's shell companies—which was of course a convoluted trail of numbered shell companies that could never lead anyone to Max— Catherine was, as Max had predicted, a very wealthy woman.

So Catherine and Stella joined forces to open the "Caress Beauty Salon." It was an immediate success since Catherine could afford to hire the best talent, combined with her Yacht Club connections and her impeccable taste and proven hostess skills. Catherine ran marketing and promotion while Stella ran the day-to-day operations, having been a sought-after hair stylist before she met John.

Trent didn't fare as well. Unfortunately for him, his mother decided he wasn't able to look after himself and moved him back into the family home where she could look after him properly.

As for Janeva and her family, with the graphene chip still in hand, murder and intrigue continue to follow them. They decide to join other Yacht Club members for a club cruise and regatta in the BVI's (British Virgin Islands). Teaming up again with Greg and Steph, they are once again into drawn into a mystery that pulls them from island to island as they sleuth out a killer and Max hunts them in his quest to recover the missing computer chip.

###

Janine Marie the author of the Rigging A Murder Series. A Canadian and enthusiastic boater, she currently lives with her family in California.

Connect Online:

Twitter: twitter.com/JanineMarieBook

Facebook: facebook.com/pages/JanineMarieBooks

Website: janinemariebooks.com/

Made in the USA
Lexington, KY
19 July 2016